EYE OF CAT

Roger Zelazny

EYE OF CAT

TIMESCAPE BOOKS

Distributed by Simon and Schuster

New York

Copyright © 1982 by The Amber Corporation
All rights reserved
including the right of reproduction
in whole or in part in any form
A Timescape Book
Published by Pocket Books, A Simon & Schuster
Division of Gulf & Western Corporation
Simon & Schuster Building
Rockefeller Center
1230 Avenue of the Americas
New York, New York 10020
Use of the trademark TIMESCAPE is by exclusive license from Gregory
Benford, the trademark owner.
Designed by Daniel Chiel
Manufactured in the United States of America

1   3   5   7   9   10   8   6   4   2

Library of Congress Cataloging in Publication Data
Zelazny, Roger.
Eye of cat.

I. Title.
PS3576.E43E9   1982   813'.54   82-10433
ISBN: 0-671-25519-3

FOR JOE LEAPHORN,
JIMMY CHEE
AND TONY HILLERMAN

PART I

At the door to the House of Darkness
  lies a pair of red coyotes with heads reversed.
Nayenezgani parts them with his dark staff
  and comes in search of me.
With lightning behind him,
  with lightning before him,
  he comes in search of me,
with a rock crystal and a talking ketahn.

Beyond, at the corners by the door
  of the House of Darkness,
lie two red bluejays with heads reversed.
With lightning behind him,
  with lightning before him,
he parts them with his dark staff
  and comes in search of me.

Farther, at the fire-pit of the Dark House,
  lie two red hoot-owls with heads reversed.
He parts these with his staff
  and comes in search of me,
  with rock crystal and talking ketahn.

At the center of the Darkness House
  where two red screech-owls lie with heads reversed,
Nayenezgani casts them aside
  coming in search of me,
  lightning behind him,
  lightning before him.
Bearing a rock crystal and a talking ketahn,
  he comes for me.
From the center of the earth he comes.

Farther . . .

Evil-Chasing Prayer

NIGHT, NEAR THE EASTERN EDGE OF
the walled, sloping grounds of the estate, within these walls, perhaps
a quarter-mile from the house itself, at the small stand of trees,
under a moonless sky, listening, he stands, absolutely silent.

Beneath his boots, the ground is moist. A cold wind tells him that
winter yields but grudgingly to spring in upstate New York. He
reaches out and touches the dark line of a slender branch to his
right, gently. He feels the buds of the fresh year's green, dreaming of
summer beneath his wide, dark hand.

He wears a blue velveteen shirt hanging out over his jeans, a wide
concha belt securing it at his waist. A heavy squash blossom
necklace—a very old one—hangs down upon his breast. High about
his neck is a slender strand of turquoise *heiche*. He has a silver
bracelet on his left wrist, studded with random chunks of turquoise
and coral. The buttons of his shirt are hammered dimes from the
early twentieth century. His long hair is bound with a strip of red
cloth.

Tall, out of place, out of time, he listens for that which may or may not become audible: indication of the strange struggle at the dark house. No matter how the encounter goes, he, William Blackhorse Singer, will be the loser. But this is his own thing to bear, from a force he set into motion long ago, a *chindi* which has dogged his heels across the years.

He hears a brief noise from the direction of the house, followed immediately by a loud crashing. This does not end it, however. The sounds continue. From somewhere out over the walls, a coyote howls.

He almost laughs. A dog, certainly. Though it sounds more like the other, to which he has again become accustomed. None of them around here, of course.

William Blackhorse Singer. He has other names, but the remembering machines know him by this one. It was by this one that they summoned him.

The sounds cease abruptly, and after a short while begin again. He estimates that it must be near midnight in this part of the world. He looks to the skies, but Christ's blood does not stream in the firmament. Only Ini, the bird of thunder among the southwestern stars, ready with his lightning, clouds and rain, extending his headplume to tickle the nose of Sas, the bear, telling him it is time to bring new life to the earth, there by the Milky Way.

Silence. Sudden, and stretching pulsebeat by pulsebeat to fill his world. Is it over? Is it really over?

Again, short barks followed by the howling. Once he had known many things to do, still knew some of them. All are closed to him now, but for the waiting.

No. There is yet a thing with which to fill it.

Softly, but with growing force, he begins the song.

Frst MAN WAS NOT EXACTLY
jumping with joy over the dark underworld in which he was created.
He shared it with eight other humans, and the ants and the beetles
and later the locusts whom they encountered as they explored, and
Coyote—the First Angry One, He-who-was-formed-in-the-water,
Scrawny Wanderer. Everyone multiplied; and the dragonflies, the
wasps and the bat people later joined them; and Spider Man and
Spider Woman. The place grew crowded and was full of bugs. Strife
ensued.

"Let's get out of here," a number of them suggested.

First Man, who was wise and powerful, fetched his treasures of
White Shell, Turquoise, Abalone, Jet and the Red-White Stone.

He placed the White Shell in the east and breathed upon it. Up
from it rose a white tower of cloud. He placed the Turquoise to the
south and breathed upon it. From it there rose a blue cloud tower.
To the west he set the Abalone, and when he had breathed upon it a
yellow cloud tower rose up in that place. To the north he set the Jet,
and touched by his breath it sent up a black tower of cloud. The
white and the yellow grew, met overhead and crossed, as did the
blue and the black. These became the Night and the Day.

Then he placed the Red-White Stone at the center and breathed
upon it. From it there rose a many-colored tower.

The tower to the east was called Folding Dawn; that to the south
was called Folding Blue Sky; to the west, Folding Twilight; that to
the north, Folding Darkness. One by one, Coyote visited each of
them, changing his color to match their own. For this reason, he is
known as Child of the Dawn, as Child of the Blue Sky, Child of the
Twilight and Child of Darkness, along with all his other names. At
each of these places, his power was increased.

While the towers of the four cardinal points were holy, giving
birth to the prayer rites, the central one bore all pains, evils and

11

diseases. And it was this tower up which First Man and Coyote led the People, bringing them into the second world; and, of course, along with them, the evils.

There they explored and they met with others, and First Man fought with many, defeating them all and taking their songs of power.

But this also was a place of suffering, of misery, a thing Coyote discovered as he went to and fro in the world and up and down it. And so to First Man he took the pleas that they depart.

First Man made a white smoke and blew it to the east, then swallowed it again—and the same in every direction. This removed all the evils from the world and brought them back to the People from whence they had come. Then he laid Lightning, both jagged and straight, to the east, and Rainbow and Sunlight, but nothing occurred. He moved them to the south, the west and the north. The world trembled but brought forth no power to bear them upward. He made then a wand of Jet, Turquoise, Abalone and White Shell. Atop this, he set the Red-White Stone. It rose and bore them upward into the next world.

Here they met the many snakes, and Salt Man and Woman and Fire God. Nor should Spider Ant be forgotten. And light and darkness came up from the towers of the four colors, as in the other worlds.

But then First Man set a streak of yellow and another of red and yellow in the east, and these halted the movement of the white light.

And the People were afraid. Salt Man counseled them to explore in the east, but the streaks retreated as they advanced. Then they heard a voice summoning them to the south. There they found the old man Dontso, called Messenger Fly, who told them what First Man had done. The yellow streak, he said, represented the emergence of the People; the other, vegetation and pollen, with the red part indicating all diseases.

Then Owl and Kit Fox and Wolf and Wildcat came, and with them Horned Rattlesnake, who offered First Man the shell he carried on his head—and promises of offerings of White Shell,

Turquoise, Abalone and Jet in the future. First Man accepted the shell and its magic and removed the streaks from the sky.

The People then realized that First Man was evil. Coyote spied upon their counsels and reported to First Man that they knew he had stopped the light in the east to gain a treasure.

When later they confronted him with it, First Man replied, "Yes. It is true, grandchildren. Very true. I am evil. Yet I have employed my evil on your behalf. For these offerings shall benefit all of us. And I do know when to withhold my evil from those about me."

And he proceeded to prove this thing by building the first medicine hogan, where he shared with them his knowledge of things good and evil.

H E REMEMBERED THE PARTY THE night before he had found the coyote.

Garbed in the rented splendor of a shimmering synthetic-fibered foursquare and blackrib Pleat & Ruffle evegarb, he had tripped through to the mansion in Arlington. Notables past and present filled the sparkling, high-ceilinged rooms. He was decidedly Past, but he had gone anyway, to see a few old friends, to touch that other life again.

A middle-aged woman of professional charm greeted him, approached him, embraced him and spoke with him for half a minute in the enthusiastic voice of a newscaster, until a fresh arrival at his back produced a reflex pressure from her hand upon his arm, directing him to the side.

Grateful, he moved off, accepting a drink from a tray, glancing at faces, nodding to some, pausing to exchange a few words, working his way to a small room he recalled from previous visits.

He sighed when he entered. He liked the wood and iron, stone and rough plaster, books and quiet pictures, the single window with its uninterrupted view of the river, the fireplace burning softly.

"I knew you'd find me here," she said, from her chair near the hearth.

He smiled.

"So did I—in the only room built during a lapse in tastelessness."

He drew up a chair, seating himself near her but facing slightly past her toward the fire. Her heavy, lined face, the bright blue eyes beneath white hair, her short stocky figure, had not changed recently. In some ways she was the older, in others she was not. Time had played its favorite game—irony—with them both. He thought of the century-old Fontenelle and Mme. Grimaud, almost as old as he. Yet there was a gulf here of a different sort.

"Will you go collecting again soon?" she asked him.

"They've all the beasties they need for a while. I'm retired."

"Do you like it?"

"As well as anything."

Her brows tightened in a small wince.

"I can never tell whether it's native fatalism, world-weariness or a pose with you."

"I can't either, anymore," he said.

"Perhaps you're suffering from leisure."

"That's about as exclusive as rain these days. I exist in a private culture."

"Really. It can't be as bad as all that," she said.

"Bad? Good and evil are always mixed up. It provides order."

"Nothing else?"

"It is easy to love what is present and desire what is absent."

She reached out and squeezed his hand.

"You crazy Indian. Do you exist when I'm not here?"

"I'm not sure," he said. "I was a privileged traveler. Maybe I died and no one had the heart to tell me. How've you been, Margaret?"

After a time, she said, "Still living in an age of timidity, I suppose. And ideas."

He raised his drink and took a big swallow.

". . . Stale, flat and unprofitable," she said.

He raised the glass higher, holding it to the light, staring through it.

"Not that bad," he stated. "They got the vermouth right this time."

She chuckled.

"Philosophy doesn't change people, does it?" she asked.

"I don't think so."

"What are you going to do now?"

"Go and talk with some of the others, I guess, have a few more drinks. Maybe dance a little."

"I don't mean tonight."

"I know. Nothing special, I guess. I don't need to."

"A man like you should be doing something."

"What?"

"That's for you to say. When the gods are silent someone must choose."

"The gods are silent," he said, finally looking into her bright ancient eyes, "and my choices are all used up."

"That's not true."

He looked away again.

"Let it be," he said, "as you did before."

"Don't."

"I'm sorry."

She removed her hand from his. He finished his drink.

"Your character is your fate," she said at last, "and you are a creature of change."

"I live strategically."

"Maybe too much so."

"Let it be, lady. It's not on my worry-list. I've changed enough and I'm tired."

"Will even that last?"

"Sounds like a trick question to me. You had your chance. If I've an appointment with folly I'll keep it. Don't try to heal my wounds until you're sure they're there."

"I'm sure. You have to find something."

"I don't do requests."

". . . And I hope it's soon."

"I've got to take a little walk," he said. "I'll be back."

She nodded and he left quickly. She would too, shortly.

Later that evening his eyes suddenly traced a red strand in the rug and he followed it, to find himself near the trip-box.

"What the hell," he said.

He sought his hostess, thanked her and moved back to the transport unit. He pushed the coordinates, and as he entered he stumbled.

Freeze frame on man falling.

There was a time when the day light was night light.
Black-god rode upon my right shoulder.
Time spun moebius about me, as I sailed
up Darkness Mountain in the sky.
And the beasts, the beasts I hunted.
When I called them they would come to me,
out of Darkness Mountain.

IT HAD SNOWED THE PREVIOUS NIGHT, dry and powdery, but the day had been unseasonably warm and much of it had melted. The sky was still clear as the sun retreated behind a dark rocky crest, and already the cold was coming back into the world, riding the wind that sighed among the pine trees. Silvery strings of sunlight marked the higher sinews of a mesa far to the right, its foot already aswirl with gray in the first tides of evening. At least there would be no snow tonight, he knew, and he could watch the stars before he closed his eyes.

As he made his camp, the coyote limped after him, its left foreleg still bound. Tonight was the night to take care of that, too.

He built his fire and prepared his meal, the piñon smoke redolent in his nostrils. By the time that it was ready the day was gone, and the mesa and the ridge were but lumps of greater darkness against the night.

"Your last free meal," he said, tossing a portion of the food to the beast at his feet.

As they ate, he remembered other nights and other camps, a long trail of them stretching back over a century. Only this time there was nothing to hunt, and in a way this pleased him.

Drinking his coffee, he thought of the hundred-seventy years of his existence: how it had begun in this place, of the fairylands and hells through which he had taken it and how he had come—back. "Home," under the circumstances, would be more than an irony. He sipped the scalding brew from the metal cup, peopling the night with demons, most of whom now resided in San Diego.

Later, with his hunting knife, he removed the dressing from the animal's leg. It remained perfectly still as he did this, watching. As he cut away at the stiff material, he recalled the day some weeks before when he had come upon it, leg broken, in a trap. There had been a time when he would have acted differently. But he had released it, taken it home with him, treated it. And even this, this long trek into the Carrizos, was for the purpose of turning it free at a sufficient distance from his home, with a full night ahead to tempt it into wandering back to its own world, rather than prolonging an unnatural association.

He slapped its flank.

"Go on. Run!"

It rose, its movements still stiff, leg still held at an awkward angle.

17

Only gradually did it lower the limb as it moved about the campsite. After a time, it passed into and out of the circle of firelight, remaining away for longer and longer periods.

As he prepared his bedroll, he was startled by a buzzing noise. Simultaneously, a red light began winking on the small plastic case which hung from his belt. He switched off the buzzer, but the light continued to blink. He shrugged and put it aside, face down. It indicated an incoming call at his distant home. He had gotten into the habit of wearing the unit when he was near the place and had forgotten to remove it. He never wore the more elaborate version, however, and so was not equipped to answer the call from here. This did not seem important. It had been several years since he had received anything which might be considered an important call.

Still, it troubled him as he lay regarding the stars. It had been a long while since he had received any calls at all. He wished now that he had either carried along the unit's other component or had not brought anything. But he was retired, his newsworthiness long vanished. It could not really be important. . . .

. . . He was traversing an orange plain beneath a yellow sky in which a massive white sun blazed. He was approaching an orange, pyramidal structure covered with a webwork of minute fractures. He drew near and halted, hurriedly setting up the projector. Then he commenced waiting, occasionally moving to tend another machine which produced a continuous record as the cracks grew. Time meant very little to him. The sun drifted slowly. Abruptly, one of the jagged lines widened and the structure opened. A wide-shouldered form covered with pink stubble rose up suddenly out of it, swaying, a raw, bristle-edged opening facing him forward of the bulbous projection at its top, beneath a dazzling red band of jewel-like knobs. He triggered the projector and a gleaming net was cast upon it. It struggled within it but could not come free. Its movements came to correspond with a faint drumming sound which might be his heartbeat. Now the entire world crashed and fell away and he was running, running into the east, younger self of his self, beneath a blue sky, past saltbush and sagebrush, clumps of scrub grass and

18

chamisa, the sheep barely noting his passage, save for one which suddenly rose up, assuming all the colors of the dawn, swaying. . . . And then everything swam away on dark currents to the places where dreams dwell when they are not being used. . . .

Birdnotes and predawn stasis: he was cast up onto the shoals of sleep, into a world where time hung flexed at the edge of light. Frozen. His emerging awareness moved slowly over preverbal landscapes of thought he had quitted long ago. Or was it yesterday?

He awoke knowing that the call was important. He tended to his morning and removed all signs of his camp before the sun was fully risen. The coyote was nowhere in sight. He began walking. It had been a long time, too long for him to go further into the portent. His feelings, however, were another matter. He scrutinized them occasionally, but seldom examined them closely.

As he hiked across the morning, he considered his world. It was small again, as in the beginning, though this was a relative matter—relative to all the worlds he had traveled in. He moved now in the foothills of the Carrizo Mountains in Dinetah, the land of the Navajos, over twenty-five thousand square miles, much of it still grazing land, over a million and a half acres still wildland, bounded by the four sacred mountains—Debentsa in the north, Mount Taylor in the south, San Francisco Peaks in the west and Blanco Peak in the east, each with its stories and sacred meanings. Unlike many things he had known, Dinetah had changed only slowly, was still recognizable in this, the twenty-second century, as the place it had been in his boyhood. Returning to this land after so many years had been like traveling backward in time.

Yet there were differences between this day and that other. For one, his clan had always been a small one, and now he found himself its last survivor. While it was true that one is born a member of one's mother's clan but in a sense is also born for one's father's clan, his father had been a Taoseño and there had been very little contact with the pueblo. His father—a tall, sinewy man, an unusually gifted tracker, with more than a little Plains blood—had come to live

19

in Dinetah, as was proper, tending his wife's flocks and hoeing her corn, until the day a certain restlessness overtook him.

Even so, it was not the lack of clan affiliation which had altered his life. A Navajo has great potential for personal contacts through the complex network of tribal interrelationships, so that even though all of the people he had known in his youth were likely dead, he might still find ready acceptance elsewhere. But he had returned with an Anglo wife and had not done this. He felt a momentary pang at the thought, though more than three years had passed since Dora's death.

It was more than that. A Navajo alone, on his own, away from the People, is said to be no longer a Navajo—and he felt that in a way this was true, though his mother, his grandmother and his great-grandmother were buried somewhere near the place where he now lived. He knew that he had changed, changed considerably, during the years away. Yet so had the People. While the land was little altered, they had lost many of the small things he remembered, small things adding up to something large. Paradoxically, then, he was on the one hand of an earlier era than his contemporaries, and on the other . . . He had walked beneath alien suns. He had tracked strange beasts, worthy of Monster-Slayer himself. He had learned the ways of the *bellicanos* and was not uncomfortable among them. There were degrees after his name, some of them earned. There was a library in his head, held firmly in the trained memory of one who had studied the chants of *yataalii.* More traditional yet more alien he found himself. He wanted to be alone, whatever he was.

He broke into an easy jog, telling himself that its purpose was to get the cold out of his bones. He ran past walls and outcrops of granite and sandstone, hillsides of piñon and juniper. Dead yuccas, their leaves touched with ice, lay like burned out stars nailed to the ground along his trail. The snow glinted on distant mountain peaks beneath a perfectly clear sky. Even after the cold had left him, he maintained his pace, deriving a kind of joy from the exertion.

The day wore on. He did not break his stride, however, until midmorning, when he halted for a brief meal upon a hillside commanding a long view down a narrow canyon where sheep grazed on dry grasses. In the distance, smoke rose from a conical, dirt-insulated hogan, its Pendleton-hung door facing him, there in the east.

An old man with a stick came out from behind a cluster of rocks, where he might have been resting while watching the sheep. Limping, he took a circuitous path which eventually brought him near.

"Yá'át'ééh," the man said, looking past him.

"Yá'át'ééh."

He asked the man to share his food, and they ate in silence for a time.

After a while, he asked the man's clan—it would have been impolite to ask his name—and learned that he was of the Rabbit Redwater People. He always found it easier to talk with the older people than the younger ones, those who lived far out rather than near the cities.

Eventually the man asked him his own clan. When he told him, the other grew silent. It is not good to talk of the dead.

"I am the last," he finally said, wanting the other to understand. "I've been away a long time."

"I know. I know the story of Star Tracker." He pushed down upon the crown of his wide-brimmed black hat as a gust of wind struck them. He looked back along the trail to the north. "Something follows you."

Still smiling at the way the old man had named him without naming him, he turned his head and looked in that direction. A large ball of tumbleweed bounced and rolled along the foot of the hill.

"Russian thistle," he said.

"No," the other replied. "Something more dangerous."

Despite his years, the fear of the *chindi* rose for a moment out of his youth. He shuddered beneath the touch of the wind.

"I see nothing else," he said.

"You have been gone for many years. Have you had an Enemy-way?"

21

"No."

"Perhaps you should."

"Perhaps I will. You know a good Enemyway singer?"

"I am a singer."

"Perhaps I will see you again on this before long."

"I have heard that Star Tracker was a singer. Long ago."

"Yes."

"When you come by again we will talk more of these things."

"Yes."

The man looked back once more, along the trail.

"In the meantime," he said, "follow a twisted path."

"I will do that."

Later, as he passed along the streaky blue shale and frozen crimson clay of a dry riverbed, naked cottonwoods flanking it like fracture lines against the cold blue of the sky, he thought of the old man's words and the things of which they reminded him—of the sky creatures and water creatures, of the beings of cloud, mist, rain, pollen and corn which had figured so prominently in his childhood imagination—here in the season when the snakes and the thunder still slept.

It had been a long while since he had considered his problems in the old terms. A *chindi* . . . Real or of the mind—what difference? Something malicious at his back. Yes, another way of looking at things . . .

The day wore on to noon and past it before the butte near his home came into view, a high-standing wind-sculpture reminiscent of something he had once seen in a seaweed-fringed valley beneath the waters of an alien ocean. He halted again at this point to eat the rest of his rations. Nature had long moods in the Southwest, he reflected, as he looked off in that direction. While it was true that the land was little altered, there had been some change between the then and the now. He could just make out stands of blue spruce near the monolith's base, a tree he had not seen in this area a century and a half ago. But then the climate had also altered somewhat during the

22

span, the winters becoming a trifle more clement, coming later, ending a bit sooner than they once had.

He filled his pipe and lit it. Shadows like multitudes of fingers stretched slowly out of the west. To run all this way, then sit and rest when the end was in sight—it seemed the thing to do. Was he afraid? he wondered. Afraid of that damned call? Maybe that was it. Or did he want a last slow-moving view of this piece of his life before something happened to change it? There had been a song. . . . He could not remember it.

When he felt that the time was proper he rose and began walking through the coolness and shadow toward the large, distant, six-sided house with the door to the east, his hogan that was not exactly a hogan.

The sky was darker by the time he reached the neighborhood of his dwelling, and the trees curtained off even more of the light, casting an as yet starless evening over the raised log-and-stucco structure. He wandered about it for several minutes before approaching from the east and mounting the rough-cut decking with which he had surrounded the place. He entered then and turned on the light. He had his own power supply, rooftop and below-ground.

Moving to the central *fogon,* he arranged some kindling and struck it to fire. He disrobed then, tossing his Levi's and red-and-white flannel shirt into a hamper along with the rest of his clothing. Crossing to a tall, narrow stall, he entered and set the timer for a three-minute UHF shower. Water was not a thing to be expended lightly in this region. When he emerged, he drew on a buckskin shirt, khaki bush pants and a pair of soft moccasins.

Activating his news recorder and display screen and adjusting it to some of his general interests, he passed to the small, open kitchen area to the right and prepared a meal, amid hanging *ristras* of chilis and onions.

He ate in a low, fur-covered chair and the walls about him were hung with rugs from Two Gray Hills and Ganado, interspersed with

23

framed photographs of alien landscapes. A rack of weapons hung on the far wall; a meter-square metal platform enclosed by shining vertical bars of varying heights stood nearby, a large console with a display screen to its right. Its message light was still blinking.

When he finished eating, he toyed with his belt unit and put it aside. He went to the kitchen and got a beer.

DISK I

CHILEAN QUAKES ABORTED

TAXTONIES ARRESTED

and three demonstrators were apprehended after reportedly setting fire to the car belonging to the official responsible for the ruling

PETROCEL DENIES PATENT INFRINGEMENT CLAIMS
"GREW OUR OWN," DIRECTOR OF RESEARCH INSISTS

EYE OF CAT

A MILD SPRING FOR MUCH OF THE NATION
EARLY FLOOD WATCHES IN MISSISSIPPI VALLEY

CHIMPANZEE COMPLAINS OF ART THEFT

References to a drugged banana figured prominently in the
bizarre statement taken today by Los Angeles detectives

KILLED THEM "BECAUSE THEY WERE THERE," MOTHER OF THREE
EXPLAINS

> *It's been a long time since you left me.*
> *Don't know what I'm gonna do.*
> *I look up at the sky and wonder—*
> *Earthlight always makes me think of you.*

COLUMBIA STUDENTS SKYDIVE FROM ORBIT TO SET NEW RECORD

"Naturally the university is proud," Dean Schlobin remarked,
"but

STRAGEAN AMBASSADOR CLOSETED WITH SECRETARY-GENERAL

25

Stragean Ambassador Daltmar Stango and Consul Orar Bogarthy continue a second day of talks with Secretary-General Walford. Speculation on a breakthrough in trade-agreement negotiations runs high, but so far the news community

W. COAST DOLPHINS PRESS CLAIMS
A-1 CANNING BELIEVED READY TO SETTLE

BAKIN M'BAWA PREDICTS END OF WORLD AGAIN

I sip the beer and hear the music,
Watch the ships as they arrive.
You packed your bag and went away, love.
I feel like H-E-L-L5.

CHURCH OF NATURAL LIFE RADICALS SUSPECTED IN SPERMOVA BANK
BOMBING

MAN SUES TO RECOVER FORMER PERSONALITY

Relying on a district court order, Menninger officials performed

BANK OF NOVA SCOTIA COMPUTER CHARGED WITH FELONY IN BONDS
MANIPULATION SCANDAL

> *Oh, I'm sittin' here and hurtin'*
> *In this slowly turnin' dive.*
> *If you ever want to reach me*
> *Just dial H-E-L-L5.*

hate   somewhere he still exists and there is no force great
enough to keep me from him forever   it has taken a long while
to learn the ways but soon i will be ready   i am
ready   eight days and had i known then what i know now he
would be gone   i would be gone   burned? burned they
say?   nevermore amid the slagheaps to chase the crawling
tubes and crunch them for their juiciness?   but this air too i
breathe and only the jagged and the straight lightnings hold me
here   i know the way beyond them now and the trees outside
the walls   visions of cities the lesser ones bear   i know the
ways i know the forms   wait   the lesser ones' twisted
minds tell me what i need   one will come one day who will
know of the one who is not like the others who still exists   i will
leave for that somewhere he exists   eight days   i died a
little he will die wholly   nothing can keep me from him
forever   i will talk first   now i know of it   words like
the crawling things   crunch them taste their
juiciness   strike now and see the lesser ones draw
back   now i know them i will use them   words   to tell
him the why of it   now i will be a sphere and roll
about   ha! lesser ones!   hate   i will talk it that
when   tell it then   eight days   burned   hate

27

$\mathbf{B}$ACK WHEN NAYENEZGANI AND HIS brother were in the process of disposing of the monsters the People had found in the new world, there were some—such as the Endless Serpent—who were, for various reasons, spared. Yet even these were tamed to a degree in their acknowledgement as necessary evils. The world was indeed becoming a safer place, though some few yet remained.

There was, for instance, Tse'Naga'Hai, the Traveling Rock, which rolled after its victims to crush and devour them. Nayenezgani traveled on a rainbow and the crooked lightning in search of it. His brother having counseled him to take the magic knives with him, he had all eight of them about his person.

When he came to the place called Betchil gai, he took out his two black knives, crossed them and planted them. Beyond, he planted the two blue knives, crosswise. Farther along, he crossed the two yellow knives and planted them. Farther yet, he planted the two knives with the serrated edges, also crosswise.

He moved then in sight of the giant Rock.

"What are you waiting for, Tse'Naga'Hai?" he asked it. "Do you not pursue my kind?"

With a crunching, grinding noise, the mossless boulder he had just addressed stirred. It moved slowly in his direction, gaining momentum noticeably after but a few moments. It almost took him by surprise with the speed with which it approached.

But he whirled and raced away. It came on rapidly at his back, gaining upon him.

When he reached the place of the serrated knives, Nayenezgani leaped over them. The Rock rolled across them and a big piece broke away.

He continued to flee, jumping over the yellow knives.

Tse'Naga'Hai rolled over them also, and another fracture occurred; more pieces fell away.

By now, the Rock was bouncing from side to side and rolling in an irregular pattern. And when Nayenezgani leaped over the blue knives and the Rock crashed into them and bounced over, more pieces fell away. By now, its size was considerably reduced though its velocity was increasing.

Nayenezgani sprang over the black knives. When he heard the Rock grating and cracking itself upon them, he turned.

All that remained was a relatively small stone. He halted, then moved toward it.

Immediately it swerved, altering its course to bound away from him. Now he pursued it into the west, beyond the San Juan River. Finally, there he caught it, and much of the life and wit seemed gone out of it.

"Now, Tse'Naga'Hai," he said, "the power to harm me is gone from you, but you are not without a certain virtue I noted earlier. In the future you will serve to light the fires of the Dineh."

He raised what remained of the Rock and bore it off with him to show to First Woman, who otherwise would not have believed what he had done.

Finally HE SIGHED AND ROSE. HE crossed to the console beside the area enclosed by the shining bars. He pushed the "Messages" button and the display screen came alive.

EDWIN TEDDERS CALLED, it read, followed by the previous day's date and the time—the time when his unit had signaled in the wilderness. Below, it listed six other attempts by Edwin Tedders to reach him, the most recent only a few hours ago. There was an eastern code and a number, and a request that he return the call as soon as possible, prefaced by the word URGENT.

He tried to recall whether he had ever known an Edwin Tedders. He decided that he had not.

He punched out the digits and waited.

The buzzing which followed was broken, but the screen remained dark.

"Yes?" came a crisp male voice.

"William Blackhorse Singer," he said, "returning Edwin Tedders's call."

"Just a moment, please." The words hurried and rose in pitch. "I'll get him."

He tugged at a turquoise earring and regarded the blank screen. A minute shuffled its numbers on a nearby clock-display. Another . . .

The screen suddenly glowed, and the heavily lined face of a dark-haired man with pale eyes appeared before him. His smile seemed one of relief rather than pleasure.

"I'm Edwin Tedders," he said. "I'm glad we finally got hold of you, Mr. Singer. Can you come through right now?"

"Maybe." He glanced at the gleaming cage to his left. "But what's this all about?"

"I'll have to tell you in person. Please reverse the transfer charges. It is important, Mr. Singer."

"All right. I'll come."

He moved to his trip-box and began its activation. It whined faintly for an instant. Zones of color moved upward within the shafts.

"Ready," he said, stepping into the unit.

Looking down, he saw that his feet were growing dim.

For a moment, the world was disarrayed. Then his thoughts fell back into place again. He was standing within a unit similar to his own. When he raised his head he looked out across a large room done up in an old-fashioned manner—dark paneled walls, heavy leather chairs, a Chinese rug, bookshelves filled with leatherbound volumes, drapes, a fireplace burning real logs. Two men stood facing him—Tedders, and a slight, blond man whose voice identified him as the one with whom he had first spoken.

"This is Mark Brandes, my secretary," Tedders stated as he watched him step down.

He inadvertently pressed his palm rather than clasping hands, in the old way of the People. Brandes looked puzzled but Tedders was already gesturing toward the chairs.

"Have a seat, Mr. Singer."

"Call me Billy."

"All right, Billy. Would you care for a drink?"

"Sure."

"I have some excellent brandy."

"That'll be fine."

Tedders looked at Brandes, who immediately moved to a sideboard and poured a pair of drinks.

"Early spring," Tedders said.

Billy nodded, accepted his glass.

"You've had a fascinating career. Both freezing and time-dilation effects kept you around till you could benefit from medical advances. A real old-timer, but you don't look it."

Billy took a sip of his brandy.

"This is very good stuff," he said.

"Yes. Real vintage. How many trackers are there around these days?"

"I don't know."

"There are others, but you're the best. Old school."

Billy chuckled.

"What do you want?" he asked.

Tedders chuckled also.

"The best," he said.

"What do you want tracked?"

"It isn't exactly that."

"What, then?"

"It's hard to know where to begin. . . ."

31

Billy looked out the window, across the moon-flooded lawn. In the distance, the prospect was broken by a high wall.

"I am a special assistant to Secretary-General Walford," Tedders finally stated. "He is here—upstairs—and so are the Stragean ambassador and consul—Stango and Bogarthy. Do you know much about the Strageans?"

"I've met a few, here and there."

"How did they strike you?"

He shrugged.

"Tall, strong, intelligent . . . What do you mean?"

"Would you want one for an enemy?"

"No."

"Why not?"

"They could be very dangerous."

"In what ways?"

"They'd be hard to stop. They're shapeshifters. They have a kind of mental control over their bodies. They can move their organs around. They can—"

"Walk through walls?"

Billy shook his head.

"I don't know about that. I've heard it said, but I've never—"

"It's true. They have a training regimen which will produce this ability in some of them. Semireligious, quite arduous, takes years, doesn't always work. But they can produce some peculiar adepts."

"Then you know more about it than I do."

"Yes."

"So why ask me?"

"One of them is on her way here."

Billy shrugged.

"There are a few thousand around. Have been for years."

Tedders sipped his drink.

"They're all normals. I mean one of those with that special training."

"So?"

32

"She's coming to kill the Secretary-General."

Billy sniffed his brandy.

"Good that you got word," he finally said, "and can turn it over to the security people."

"Not good enough."

Throughout the conversation, Tedders had been struggling to obtain eye-contact. At last Billy was staring at him, and he felt some small sense of triumph, not realizing that this meant the man doubted what he was saying.

"Why not?"

"They're not equipped to deal with Stragean adepts," he said. "She could well be too much for them."

Billy shook his head.

"I don't understand why you're telling me about it."

"The computer came up with your name."

"In response to what?"

"We'd asked it for someone who might be able to stop her."

Billy finished his drink and set the glass aside.

"Then you need a new programmer or something. There must be a lot of people who know more about Stragean adepts than I do."

"You are an expert on the pursuit and capture of exotic life forms. You spent most of your life doing it. You practically stocked the Interstellar Life Institute single-handed. You—"

Billy waved his hand.

"Enough," he said. "The alien you are talking about is an intelligent being. I spent much of my life tracking animals—exotic ones, to be sure, some very crafty and with tricky behavior patterns— but animals nevertheless, not creatures capable of elaborate planning."

Cat . . .

". . . So I don't see that my experience is really applicable in this situation," he concluded.

Tedders nodded.

"Perhaps, and perhaps not," he said at last. "But in a matter like

33

this we should really be certain. Will you talk with the Stragean representatives who are visiting here? They can probably give you a clearer picture than I can."

"Sure. I'll talk to anybody."

Tedders finished his drink and rose.

"May I get you another of those?"

"All right."

He replenished the snifter. Then, "I'll be back in a few minutes," he said, and he moved off to the right and departed the room.

Billy set down the glass and rose. He paced the room, regarded the titles on the bookshelves, felt the volumes' spines, sniffed the air. Mingled with the smell of old leather, a faint, almost acrid aroma he had not been able to place earlier came to him again, a scent he had experienced upon meeting Strageans in the past, in another place. They must have been about this building for some time, he decided, or have been in this room very recently, to mark it so with their presence. He remembered them as humanoid, over two meters in height, dark-skinned save for silvery faces, necks and breasts; flat-headed, narrow-waisted beings with wide shoulders, collarlike outgrowths of spiny material which served as sound-sensors and small, feral eyes, slitted, usually yellow but sometimes cinnamon or amber in color; hairless, graceful in a many-jointed, insectlike way, they moved quietly and spoke a language that reminded him vaguely of Greek, which he did not understand either.

It is language, he decided, that sets the sentients apart from the animals. Isn't it?

Cat . . . ?

He moved to the window, stared out across the lawn. Difficult to cross there without being detected, he concluded, with even the simplest security devices in operation. And this place must have plenty. But she could assume almost any guise, could penetrate the place in an innocuous form. . . .

Why be furtive, though? That is what they would be expecting. While the defenders were concentrating on the sophisticated, why not hijack a heavy vehicle, come barreling across the lawn, crash through a wall, jump down from the cab and start shooting everything that moves?

He shook himself and turned away. This was not his problem. There must be plenty of people more qualified than himself to second-guess the alien, no matter what the computer said.

He returned to his chair and took up his drink. Footsteps were approaching now from the direction in which Tedders had departed. Footsteps, and the soft sound of voices, accompanied by a faint ringing in his ears. The language of the Strageans ranged into the ultrasonic on the human scale, and though they narrowed their focus when speaking Terran tongues there were always some overtones. Too long a conversation with a Stragean normally resulted in a headache. He took another drink and lowered the glass as they rounded the corner.

The two Strageans wore dark blue kilts and belts which crossed their breasts like bandoliers. Ornamental pins or badges of office were affixed to these latter. Between Tedders and the aliens walked another man, short, heavy, with just a fringe of dark hair; his eyes were jadelike under heavy brows; he wore a green robe and slippers. Billy recognized him as UN Secretary-General Milton Walford.

Tedders introduced him to Daltmar Stango and Orar Bogarthy as well as to Walford. Everyone was seated then, and Tedders said, "They will tell you more about this."

Billy nodded.

The Stragean known as Daltmar Stango, staring at nothing directly before him, recited: "It has to do with the coming of your people to stay on our world. There is already a sizable enclave of them there, just as there is of our kind here on Earth. There has been very little trouble on either world because of this. But now, with my present mission to negotiate political and trade agreements, it appears that the settlements will become permanent diplomatic posts."

He paused but a moment, as if to refocus his thoughts, and then continued: "Now, there is a small religious group on Strage which believes that when Terrans die there, their life essences foul the

35

place of the afterlife. Permanent posts will guarantee that this group's fears will be realized with increasing frequency as time goes on. Hence, they are against any agreements with your people, and they would like all of them off our world."

"How large a group are they?" Billy asked.

"Small. Fifty to a hundred thousand members, at most. It is not their size which is important, though. They are an austere sect, and many of them undertake a severe course of training which some-times produces spectacular effects in the individual."

"So I've heard."

"One such individual has taken it upon herself to correct matters. She commandeered a vessel and set a course for Earth. She feels that an assassination at this level will disrupt our negotiations to the point where there will be no treaty—and that this will lead to the withdrawal of Terrans from our world."

"How close is she to the truth?"

"It is always difficult to speculate in these matters, but it would certainly slow things down."

"And she's due to arrive in a few days?"

"Yes. We received the information from other members of her sect, and they could not be more precise. They did not learn the story in its entirety until after her departure, when they informed the authorities. They were anxious that it be known she was acting on her own initiative and not under orders."

Billy smiled.

"Who can say?" he said.

"Yes. At any rate, since a message can travel faster than a ship, the warning was sent."

"You must know best how to stop one of your own people."

"The problem seldom occurs," Daltmar said. "But the customary method is to set a team of similarly endowed adepts after a wrongdoer. Unfortunately . . ."

"Oh."

"So we must make do with what is at hand," the alien went on. "Your people will try to intercept her in space, but projections only give them a twenty-seven percent chance of success. Have you any ideas?"

Cat?

"No," Billy replied. "If it were a dangerous animal, I'd want to study it in its habitat for a time."

"There is no way and no time."

"Then I don't know what to tell you."

Walford produced a small parcel from the pocket of his robe.

"There is a chip in here that I want you to take back with you and run through your machine," he said. "It will tell you everything we know about this individual and about others of that sort. It is the closest thing we can give you to a life study."

Billy rose and accepted the package.

"All right," he said. "I'll take it home and run it. Maybe something will suggest itself."

Walford and the others rose to their feet. As Billy turned toward the transporter, the Stragean called Orar Bogarthy spoke.

"Yours is one of the aboriginal peoples of this continent?" he said.

"Yes," Billy replied, halting but not turning.

"Have the jewels in your earlobes a special significance? Religious, perhaps?"

Billy laughed.

"I like them. That's all."

"And the one in your hair?"

Billy touched it as he turned slowly.

"That one? Well . . . it is believed to protect one from being struck by lightning."

"Does it work?"

"This one has. So far."

"I am curious. Being struck by lightning is not the most common occurrence in life. Why do you wear it?"

"We Navajos have a thing about lightning. It destroys taboos. It twists reality. Not a thing to fool around with."

He turned away, moved ahead, punched a series of numbers, stepped up into the unit. He glanced up at the expressionless humans and aliens as the delay factor passed and his body began to melt.

> *Traveling the distance from hill to hill,*
> *passing from place to place as the wind passes,*
> *trackless. There should be a song for it,*
> *but I have never learned the words.*
> *So I sing this one of my own making:*
> *I am become a rainbow, beginning there*
> *and ending here. I leave no mark*
> *upon the land between as I arc*
> *from there to here. May I go in beauty.*
> *May it lie before, behind, above and below,*
> *to the right and the left of me.*
> *I pass cleanly through the gates of the sky.*

W E CALL IT THE ENEMYWAY, THE OLD man said, but the white people came along and started calling it a squaw dance—probably because they saw the women dancing for it. You get a special name if you're the one they're going to sing over, a warrior's name. It's a sacred name you're just supposed to use in ceremonials, not the kind you go around telling everybody or just letting people call you by.

It all started, he said, back when Nayenezgani was protecting the People. He killed off a whole bunch of monsters that were giving us a hard time. There was the Horned Monster and Big God and the Rock Monster Eagle and the Traveling Rock and a lot of others. That was why he got to be called Monster-Slayer. His fourth monster, though, was called Tracking Bear. It was a bear, but it looked more like a lion the size of a floatcar. Once it came across your tracks, it would start following them and it wouldn't stop until it had found you and had you for dinner on the spot.

Nayenezgani went out and tracked the tracker and then let it track him. But when it finally found him, he was ready. He wasn't called Monster-Slayer for nothing. When it was all over, the world was that much safer.

But at about that time, it started to get to him. He suffered for it because of all those enemies he killed, and the bear just added another one to their band. Their spirits followed him around and made him pretty miserable. This is where the word *Anaa'ji,* for the Enemyway, comes from. *Naayéé'* means an enemy, or something really bad that's bothering you. Now, *neezghání* means "he has gotten rid of it," and *ana'i* means an enemy that's been gotten rid of. So *Anaa'ji* is probably really the best word to call it by. It's a ceremony for getting rid of really bad troubles.

H E PACED. THE SCREEN STILL glowed. He had not turned off the unit after viewing the chip. The walls seemed to lean toward him, to press in upon him. The wind was singing a changing song he almost understood. He paused at various times, to inspect an old basket, an ancient flaked spear point, the photograph of a wild landscape beneath an indigo sky. He touched the barrel of a high-powered rifle, took the weapon into his hands, checked it, replaced it on its pegs. Finally he turned on his heel and stepped outside into the night.

He stood upon the decking which surrounded the hogan. He peered into the shadows. He looked up at the sky.

"I have no words . . ." he began, and a part of his mind mocked the other part. He was, as always, conscious of this division. When it had first occurred he could no longer say.

". . . But you require an answer."

He was not even certain what it was that he addressed. The Navajo language has no word for "religion." Nor was he even certain that that was the category into which his feelings fell. Category? The reason there was no word was that in the old days such things had been inextricably bound to everything in one's life. There was no special category for certain sentiments. Most of those around him even now did not find this strange. But they had changed. He had also, though he knew that his alteration was of a different order. "He behaves as if he had no relatives"—this was the worst thing one Navajo might say of another, and he knew that it applied to him. The gulf was deeper than his absence, his marriage, anything he had done. Others had gone away for long times, had married outside the clans, and had still come back. But for him it was part of a temporal experience, literally as well as spiritually true. He had no relatives. A part of him wanted it that way. The other part . . .

"I may have done a great wrong," he continued. "If I took him from his land, as the People were taken to Fort Sumner. If I took him from his own kind, who are no more. If I left him alone in a strange place, like a captive among the Utes. Then I have done a wrong. But only if he is a real person." He scanned the skies. "May he not be," he said then. "May it all be a dream of possibility, a nothingness—that which has troubled me across the years." He circled the hogan, staring off into the trees. "I had thought that not knowing was best—which may make me a coward. Yet I would have gone on this way for the rest of my days. Now—"

An owl fled past him, making a soft whooing noise.

An evil omen, a part of his mind decided, *for the owl is the bird of death and ill things.*

An owl, the other part affirmed. *They hunt at night. It is nothing more.*

40

"We have heard one another," he called after the bird. "I will find out what I have done and know what I must do."

He went back inside and reached up among cobwebs to where a key hung from a *viga*. He took it into his hand and rubbed it. He ran his finger along it as if it were as unusual an item as the spear point. Then, abruptly, he dropped it into his pocket. He crossed the room and switched off the glowing screen.

Turning, he then stepped among the bars of the trip-box, activated the control unit and punched a code. He focused his eyes upon the red Ganado rug and watched it turn pink and go away.

Darkness amid the tiny streetlights, and the sound of crickets outside the booth . . .

He stepped out of the shelter and sniffed the damp air. Large, shadow-decked trees; enviable quantities of grass furring hillsides; heavy, squat, monolithic buildings, dark now, save for little entranceway lights providing tiny grottoes which only accentuated the blackness elsewhere; no people in sight.

He moved along the sidewalk, crossed the street, cut up a hillside. There were guards about, but he avoided them without difficulty. Balboa Park was quiet now, its spectacles closed to the public until morning. The lights of San Diego and the traffic along its trailways were visible from various high points he crossed, but these seemed distant, part of another world. He moved soundlessly from shadow to shadow. He had chosen a public booth he had sometimes liked to use long ago, when he had come on normal, daytime business, enjoying the walk rather than tripping directly into the place with which he was associated. That place, of course, was now closed for the night, its trip-box also shut down.

For fifteen minutes he continued his trek, climbing and hiking toward the vast, sprawling complex that was the Interstellar Life Institute. He avoided sidewalks, parking lots and roads as much as possible. Mixed animal smells from the San Diego Zoo were occasionally borne to him in open areas by vagrant currents of wind.

Rich and jungley, the smells of some of the zoo foliage also came to him. These sensations stirred memories of other exotic creatures in other places. He recalled the capture of the wire-furred wullabree in a pen of ultrasonics, the twilpa in an ice pit, four outan in a vortex of odors. . . .

The ILI complex came into sight and he slowed. For a long while he stood halted, simply watching the place. Then, slowly, he circled it, pausing often to watch again.

Finally he stood at the rear of the building near a small parking lot containing but a single car. He crossed and used his key in the door of the employees' entrance which adjoined it.

Inside, he moved without the need for light, traversing a series of corridors, then mounting a small stair. He came to a watchman's station he remembered, then used his passkey to let himself into a nearby maintenance supply closet. There he waited for twenty minutes until a uniformed old man shuffled by, halted, inserted a key into the alarm unit and moved on.

Shortly thereafter, he emerged and entered the first hall. Some of the life units at either hand were eerily illuminated, simulating the natural lighting cycles of their inhabitants' homes, tinged by odd atmospheric compounds or reflecting meteorological peculiarities necessary for the creatures' well-being. He passed drifting gas balloons, crawling coral branches, slimy Maltese crosses, pulsating liver-colored logs, spiny wave-snakes, a Belgarde simoplex gruttling in its tangle-hole, a striped mertz, a pair of divectos, a compacted tendron in a pool of ammonia. The stalked eyes of a wormsa marakye followed his passage as they had that day on the wind barrens when it had almost collected him. He did not pause to return this regard, nor to inspect any of those others he knew so well.

He traversed the entire hall, departed it, entered another. The faint hum of generators was with him always. Despite the hermetic quality of the life units, unusual odors reached him from somewhere. He ignored all of the signs, knowing what they said. The specimens in this second hall were larger, fiercer-looking than those in the one through which he had just passed. Here he glanced at several with something almost like affection, muttering quietly in the language of the People. He began humming very softly as he entered the third hall.

After only a few paces, he began to slow.

Rocks on a plain of fused silicates . . . No visible partition between that place and the rest of the hall, as in a few others he had passed. Atmospheric equivalence . . .

He continued to slow. He halted.

A weak, pointless light suffused that plain. He seemed to hear a sighing sound.

His humming ceased and his mouth grew dry.

"I have come," he whispered, and then he approached the exhibit placarded TORGLIND METAMORPH.

Sand and rock. Yellow and glassy and orange. Streaks of black. Nothing stirred.

"Cat . . . ?" he said.

He drew nearer and continued to stare. It was no use. Even his eyes could not tell for certain. It was not just the lighting.

"Cat?"

He searched his memory of the manner in which the display had originally been set up. Yes. That rock, to the left . . .

The rock moved, even as he recalled the disposition of the environment. It rolled toward the center. It changed shape, growing more spherical as it negotiated a dip.

"There is a thing I must say, a thing I must try to do. . . ."

It elongated, unfolded a pair of appendages, propped itself upon them.

"I have wondered, wondered whether you might really under-stand me, if I tried—hard enough."

It grew another pair of appendages toward its rearward extremity, formulated a massive head, a fat, triangular tail.

"If you know anyone, you know me. I brought you here. The scars of our battle have been erased from my body, but none gave me a greater fight than yourself."

Its outline flowed. It became sleek and glistening, a thing of

43

rippling cords beneath a glassy surface. Its head developed a single faceted eye at its center.

"I have come to you. I must know whether you have understanding. For a time I thought that you might. But you have never shown it since. Now I must know. Is there sense in that brute head of yours?"

The creature stretched and turned away from him.

"If you can communicate with anyone, in any fashion, let it be me, now. It is very important."

It paced across the area toward his right.

"It is not just idle curiosity that brings me here. Give me some sign of intelligence, if you possess it."

It looked at him for a moment through that cold, unblinking gem at its head's center. Then it turned away once again, its color darkening until it could go no further. Coal, inky, absolute blackness filled its outline.

The shadow slid away toward the rear of the area and vanished.

"In a way, you have pleased me," he said then. "Good-bye, great enemy."

He turned, headed back through the hall.

Billy Blackhorse Singer. Man of the People. Last warrior of your kind. You have taken your time in coming.

He halted. He stood absolutely still.

Yes. The words come into your head. I can formulate some likeness of a human tongue and utter them if I choose, but we may as well be more intimate, who are closer than friends, farther than affection.

Cat?

That is right. Just think it. I will know. Cat serves well to name me— a lithe and independent creature, alien in sentiments. I read only the thoughts you choose to surface, not your entire mind. You must tell me all of the things you wish for me to know. Why have you come?

To see whether you are what I now see you to be.

That is all?

It has bothered me that you might be so. Why did you not communicate sooner?

44

*At first I could not. My kind transmitted only images—of the hunt—
to others like ourselves. But the power slowly grew as I regarded the
thoughts of those who came to view me this half-century past. Now I
know much of your world and your kind. You, though—you are
different from the others.*

In what way?

Like me, a predator.

*Cat! Why did you not tell someone, once you knew how, that you
are a sentient, intelligent being?*

I have learned many things. And I have been waiting.

For what?

*I have learned hate. I have been waiting for the chance to escape, to
track you as you once tracked me, to destroy you.*

*It need not have gone this far. I am sorry for the pain I have caused
you. Now that we know what you are, amends can be made.*

*The sun of my world has since gone nova. The world and all others
of my kind are no more. I have seen this in the minds of my attendants.
How can you restore it to me?*

I cannot.

*I have learned hate. I did not know hate before I came to this place.
The predator does not hate the prey. The wolf actually loves the sheep,
in its way. But I hate you, Billy Blackhorse Singer, for what you have
done to me, for having turned me into a thing. This sophistication I
learned from your own kind. Since then I have lived only for the day
when I might tell you this and act upon it.*

I am sorry. I will speak with the people who run this place.

*I will not respond to them. They will think you demented in your
allegations.*

Why?

That is not my wish. I have told you my wish.

He turned back toward the area, moving to the place where force
fields contained the dark, larger-than-man-sized creature which now
sat nearby, studying him.

*I do not see how your wishes will be realized, but I am willing to try
to help you in any other way.*

45

I see something.

What do you mean?

I see that you want something of me.

It is nothing, I now realize, that you would care to give.

Try me.

I came to learn whether I had wronged you.

You have.

To see whether you are truly intelligent.

I am.

To ask your assistance, then, in preventing a political assassination.

There followed something like laughter—hollow, without humor.

Tell me about it.

He described the situation. There was a long silence when he had finished.

Then, *Supposing I were to locate this being and thwart her? What then?*

Your freedom would of course be restored to you. There would be reparations, probably a reward, a new home. Some equivalent world might be found. . . .

The dark form rose, changing shape again, becoming bearlike, bipedal. It extended a forelimb until it came into contact with the field. A rush of sparks cascaded about the area.

That, Cat told him, *is all that stands between you and death.*

That is all you have to say—that now that we can communicate we have nothing to talk about?

Do you not recall that long week you stalked me?

Yes.

It was only by a fluke that you captured me.

Perhaps.

Perhaps? You know it is so. I almost had you there at the end.

You came close.

I have relived that hunt for fifty long years. I should have won!

He slammed against the field and sparks outlined his entire figure. Billy did not move. After a time, Cat drew back, shaking himself. He seemed smaller now, and his body coiled around and around upon itself, sinking to the ground.

Finally, *You have already offered me my liberty, without conditions,* Cat said.

Yes.

The reward and reparations of which you spoke mean nothing to me.

I see.

No, you do not.

I see that you will not help in this. Very well. Good night to you.

He turned away again.

I did not say that I would not help.

When he looked back it was a swaying, hooded, horned thing which regarded him.

What is it that you do say, Cat?

I will help you—for a price.

And what is that price?

Your life.

Preposterous.

I have waited this long. It is the only thing that I want.

It is an insane offer.

It is my only offer. Accept it or not, as you choose.

Do you really think you can stop a Stragean adept?

If I fail and she destroys me, then you are free and no worse off than before. But I will not fail.

It is unacceptable.

Again the laugh.

Billy Singer turned and walked from the hall. The laughter followed him. Its range was approximately a quarter of a mile.

DISK II

BODY OF UNION LEADER FOUND IN ORBIT

Would have been incinerated upon reentry several days

EIGHTEEN INDICTED IN LUNAR DEALS

GULF HURRICANE ABORTED

he climbed Mount Taylor, birthplace of Changing Woman, sacred peak of the turquoise south. The clouds were heavy in the north, but the sun shone to his left. A cold wind sang a fragile song. He cast a pinch of pollen to each of the world's four quarters. As his existential mood deepened a *yei* came to him in the form of a drifting black feather

GENEFIX–REVLON MERGER HINTED

EYE OF CAT

EUTHANASIA VICTIM TELLS ALL

CALL FOR PARANORMALS

The UN Secretary-General's office early this morning

. . . I feel like H-E-L-L5!

CHURCH OF CHRISTIAN RELATIVITY TAKES STAND

Her sensors held as the ship banked. Running the defense system would not be so difficult after all, her instruments informed her. She meditated for half a minute upon the flame and the water, visible mutabilities symbolizing the change-flame. Flow, she imaged, into the ancient forms

FLOODING IN L.A.–PHOENIX TUNNEL
MAN CARRIED TWO MILES

"Your horses are yours again, grandchild," he says as he sits down beside me.

"Your sheep are yours again, grandchild," he says as he sits down beside me.

"All your possessions are yours again, grandchild," he says as he sits down beside me.

"Your country is yours again, grandchild," he says as he sits down beside me.

"Your springs that flow are yours again, grandchild," he says as he sits down beside me.

"Your mountain ranges are yours again, grandchild," he says as he sits down beside me.

. . .

Blessed again it has become, blessed again it has become,
Blessed again it has become, blessed again it has become!

He HAD CROSSED THE DRIED LAVA flow, which in his day everyone had known to be the congealed blood of Yeitso, a monster slain by Nayenezgani. And then he had continued upward along the slopes of Mount Taylor, its heights hidden today by a great, rolling bank of fog. A nagging wind clutched at his garments with many hands, a black wind from out of the north. A holy place was necessary for the thoughts he wished to think on this bleak day. It had been over a century since he had visited Mount Taylor, but its nature was such that it had been left undisturbed through all these years.

Climbing . . .

Cat my chindi . . . *Ever at my back* . . .

Climbing, his hair gleaming from a recent shampoo with yucca roots . . .

. . . All things past come together in you.

50

Climbing, into the fog now, the wind abruptly dying, stones dark and slippery . . .

. . . *And how shall I face you?*

. . . *Mountain held to the earth by a great stone knife, pierced through from top to bottom, female mountain, you have seen all things among the People. But do you know the stranger stars I have looked upon? Let me tell you of them. . . .*

The climb was slow and the mists pressed upon him, dampening his garments until they clung. He sang as he ascended, pausing at several places, for this was the home of Turquoise Boy and Yellow Corn Girl, and in some versions of the story it was here that Changing Woman had been born.

. . . *I have lost myself among bright stars.*

He passed a group of stone people who seemed to nod behind their veil of mist. The fleecy whiteness which surrounded him made him think of his mother's sheep, which he had herded as a boy. His thoughts followed them from their old winter hogan, its forage exhausted, to the high summer camp, where meals were cooked and eaten outdoors and the women set up their looms between the trees. His uncle, the singer, would gather herbs and dry them in the sun. The old man held a medicine bundle for Female Shootingway, of the five-night chantway. He also did the five-night Blessingway chant and knew minor Shootingway ceremonies, as well as the five nights of Evilway. And he knew the Restorationway of every living thing.

When the word came that the government inspectors were waiting at the sheep-dips, a festive spirit danced among the settlements like a humpbacked piper. The camp was broken, and the sheep bells clunked as the animals were herded down from the mountains to the place of the dips. The dips themselves stank of sulphur, and the smell of sheep dung was everywhere, not least of all upon one's boots. It was a slow, dirty business, as the sheep were run through the dips one by one, counted, collected together, certified as free of ticks and disease for another season. The air was filled with dust

51

from the moving animals. Soon flocks of them covered the hills like fallen clouds, barking dogs moving among them.

As the day progressed, a holiday atmosphere would spread among the stench and the noises. The smells of mutton stew, fry bread and coffee, mingled with the fragrance of piñon smoke, began to move through the air. Laughter would rise with greater frequency. Gambling would begin. Songs would be heard. Here or there, a horse race, a chicken-pull . . .

And the garments would improve as the work was done. The woman who might have worn a wool shawl and carried a sun umbrella while herding her sheep from the pen to the dip now had on her best bright three-tiered skirt, a satin shirt and velvet overblouse with silver collar points and silver buttons running down each shoulder seam to the wrist, silver bowknot buttons down the front, a heavy squash blossom necklace, several strands of turquoise within it. The men appeared in velveteen shirts with silver buttons, silver and turquoise bands about their black hats, green and blue bracelets, rings, necklaces—from Pilot Mountain, Morinci, Kingman, Royston. And there were jokes and dancing, though no stories of the supernatural variety, for the thunder and the serpents were awake. He remembered his first squaw dance on such an occasion. He had had nothing with which to pay, and so he had danced and danced for most of the night, listening to the girls' laughter, moving finally like a man in a dream, until an opportunity—perhaps intentional?—presented itself, and he fled.

And now . . .

This past summer he had visited a contemporary sheep-dipping. The genetically tailored animals were immune to most of the old diseases. Still, a few parasites could cause annoyance. The sheep were run through a quickly assembled, lightweight, odorless aerosol tunnel, counted and sorted by computer and penned behind a series of UHF walls broadcast from tiny units dropped casually upon the ground. For the most part, meals were prepared in quick, efficient—if a bit old-fashioned—portable microwave units. The evening's music was chip-recorded or satellite-broadcast. Most of the dancing that followed he did not recognize. There seemed to be fewer traditional garments in sight, fewer people doing things in the right manner. Not too many horses about. And a young man actually came up to him and asked him his name. . . .

. . . *Mountain held to the earth by a great stone knife, pierced through from top to bottom, blade decorated with turquoise, color of the blue south, female mountain, upon your summit a bowl of turquoise containing two bluebird eggs covered with sacred buckskin, mountain dressed in turquoise, eagle plumes upon your head, you have seen all things among the People. For a man, however, to see too much of change may damage his spirit. I have seen much. . . .*

He climbed a lightening way, through the houses made of dark cloud, rainbow and crystal. When he emerged onto the high slopes, into brightness beneath an unscreened sun, it was as if he stood upon an island in the midst of a frothing sea. The land was covered over in every direction by a cottony whiteness. He faced each of the world's corners and he sang, making offerings of cornmeal and pollen. Then he seated himself and opened his unwounded deerskin pouch, removing certain items. For a long while he thought upon the things that came to him then. . . .

That line of clouds . . . so like a curved dirt altar. A mushroom in its nest upon it. Night. He had eaten the bitter medicine and listened to the singing and the drumming. The rattle and the feather fan were passed. Each person sang four songs before handing on the regalia. A feeling of extreme weariness had come over him even before it was his turn. He understood that John Rave had once said that this was the effect of the peyote struggling against a person's vices. His throat felt constricted and very dry. He wondered how much of this was spiritual and how much physiological.

He had been going through a very unusual period in his life. He had been away to school. The old ways no longer seemed right, but neither did the new ones. He understood that the Native American Church had appealed to many who felt themselves between worlds. But he had also, already, taken anthropology courses, and he felt a thin edge of estrangement—like a knifeblade—inserting itself

53

between him and the experience even now, after only a few weeks of Peyoteway. The brilliantly colored hallucinations were often fascinating, yet he and his thirst had stood apart.

But this night was somehow different from other nights. . . . He felt this as he passed the rattle and the fan and, looking up, saw that a rainbow was forming. It did not seem at all out of place, and he watched it with interest. It seemed simultaneously distant and near, and as he stared there was movement upon it. Two figures—and he knew them—were passing along its crest as upon the arch of a great bridge. They halted and looked down at him. They were the Warrior Twins—Tobadzischini, Born-of-Water, and Nayenezgani, Monster-Slayer. For a long while they simply stared, and then he realized that it might not really be himself that they were regarding. From a sudden movement, he became aware of a great black bird, a raven, perched upon his left shoulder. Fleetingly, beneath the rainbow, a coyote passed. Nayenezgani strung his bow with lightning and raised it, but his brother placed his hand upon his arm and he lowered it.

When he looked again to his left, the raven had vanished. When he returned his gaze forward, the rainbow was smaller, fading. . . .

The next day he was weak, and he rested and drank liquids. His thought processes seemed sluggish. But the vision was somehow very important. The more he examined it the more puzzling it became. Was it the raven that Nayenezgani had been about to shoot, or was it himself? Was the bird protecting him against the Warrior Twins? Or were the brothers trying to protect him from the bird?

In the light of his recent anthropological studies, it became even more involved. Raven did figure in some of the People's stories— particularly around the Navajo Mountain, Rainbow Bridge, Piute Canyon area—as a demonic force. Yet this had not always been so, though the time when things were otherwise lay beyond the memory of anyone alive.

Raven was a principal deity among the Tlingit-Haida people of the Pacific Northwest, and these people spoke a language of the Athabascan group. The Navajo and their relatives, the Apache, also spoke an Athabascan tongue and were the only people to do so

54

outside the Northwest. In ancient times there had been a migration which had finally led the People to the canyons and mesas of Arizona, Utah, Colorado, New Mexico. In the days of their wanderings they had followed hunters' deities, such as Raven, Mountain Lion and Wolf, who had accompanied them on the long trek southward. But the People had changed when they had settled, attaching themselves to a particular area, learning agriculture from the Zuni and the Pueblo, weaving from the Hopi and, later, sheepherding from the Spaniard. With the passing of a way of life, gods of the old days were eclipsed. Raven—or Black-god, as he was now known—had even fought an inconclusive duel with Nayenezgani between San Francisco Peaks and Navajo Mountain. So Raven was a figure out of the very distant past. He had been honored when the People had been hunters rather than herders, farmers, weavers, silversmiths.

The Peyoteway, he knew, was an even newer thing, learned from the Utes. And it was new, in many ways, also for those who were lost, though it might touch upon ancient chords. The crossed lines on the ground behind the altar were said to be the footprints of Christ. He chose to regard them as giant bird-tracks. He knew that he would never go back to the Peyote hogan, for this way was not his way, though it had served to bring him an important message. For good or ill, he saw that he was marked to be a hunter.

He would finish school and he would learn the songs his uncle wished to teach him. He knew without knowing how he knew that both of these things would be important in the hunting he must one day do. He would venerate the old ways yet learn the new—the very old ways, and the very new—and in this there was no contradiction, for a Navajo was one of the most adaptable creatures on Earth. The nearby Hopis danced and prayed for rain. His people did not. They sought to live with their environment rather than to control it. The Pueblos, the Zunis, the Hopis lived clustered together like *bellicanos* in condominiums. His people did not. They lived apart from one another and families took care of themselves. Other tribes incorporated *bellicano* words into their languages to explain new things. Even in the twentieth century the Navajo language had evolved to cover the changing times, with over two hundred new words just to name the various parts of the internal combustion engine. They had learned from the Anglos, the Spaniards, the Pueblos, the Zunis, the Hopis. They had flowed, they had adapted, yet had remained themselves. Not for nothing did they consider themselves descendants of Changing Woman.

Yes. He would learn both the new and the old, he had told himself. And Black-god would accompany him on the hunt.

And this had come to pass. Yet he had not counted on so much change on the part of the People in the time-twisted times he had been away. They were still the People, different from all others. But their rate of change and his had been different.

Now, looking across the world from atop Mount Taylor, he saw that Black-god, who had chosen him, had kept his promise, making him into the mightiest hunter of his time. But now he was retired and those days were past. It seemed too much of an effort for an individual to adapt any further. The People as a whole were an organic thing and had had much time to adjust, slowly. Let it be. His design was drawn. Perhaps it was right to walk away from it now in beauty and die like the legend he had become.

He began the mountaintop song for this place. The staccato words rolled out across his world.

As the day wore on the clouds became colored smoke below him. Something passed overhead, uttering a single cawing note. Later he discovered a black feather which had fallen nearby. As he added it to his *jish* in the unwounded deerskin pouch, he wondered at its ambiguous character. Black, the color of the north, the direction in which the spirits of the departed travel. Black north, from which the *chindi* returns, along with other evil things. Black for north, for death. Yet Raven might cast a black feather, send it to him. And what might that imply?

Whatever . . . Though he could not read its depths, he could see its surface. He drew circles in the dust with his forefinger, and then he rubbed them out. Yes. He knew.

But still he sat there, on his island in the sky, and the day drifted through noon. Finally the call he had been expecting came. He knew that it would be Edwin Tedders before he heard the voice.

"Billy, we are getting very nervous here. Have you gone over the data?"

"Yes."

"Did you come up with anything?"

"Yes."

"Can you trip through now?"

"No. There's no box anywhere near here."

"Well, get to one! We've got to know, and I don't want it on the phone."

"Can't do that," he said.

"Why not?"

"If the lady in question numbers among her other virtues the ability of knowing what people have on their minds, I don't want her getting this from you."

"Wait a minute. I'll call you back."

A little later, the second call came through.

"Okay. This is the tightest fit. Listen, Targetman will be a skip and a jump away from a box to no one here knows where. And it blows immediately after tripping."

"If she can kill its juice—"

"Maybe yes, maybe no. We're also calling in human psis."

"There aren't all that many and they aren't all predictable. Right?"

"A few are very good. And some are here already."

"They find you anything?"

"Nothing yet. Now, what do you have in mind? Can you state it in such a general fashion that we'll have an idea without details she can use?"

"No."

There was a pause. Then, "Christ! We've got to have *something*, Billy! We might be falling over each other."

"You won't even know I'm around."

"You *will* be in the area?"

"No details, remember? Your own psis might even get it from you—then she might get it from them if she misses you."

"If you're going to be in the neighborhood a psi might just as easily get it from you."

"I don't think so. Primitive people can sometimes go black on a telepath. I've seen it happen on other worlds. I've gone primitive again."

"Well, how soon will you be on the job?"

Billy regarded the sinking sun.

"Soon," he said.

"You can't just state simply what you're going to do?"

"We're going to stop her."

"You've become royalty or an editor? Or acquired a tapeworm? What's this 'we'? You have to let us know if you're bringing other people in on this."

"I'm not bringing other people in on it."

"Billy, I don't like this—"

"Neither do I, but it will be done. You won't be able to reach me after this."

"Well, good-bye. . . . That's it, then. Good luck."

"Good-bye."

He faced the white east, the blue south, the yellow west and the black north and bade them good-bye; also, the Holy People of the mountain. Then he climbed back from one world to the other.

> *The Iroquois called you*
> *the Being without a Face.*
> *I go to look and see if this is true,*
> *great Destroyer*
> *who goes about menacing*
> *with couched lance and raised hatchet.*
> *I put my feet down with pollen*
> *as I walk.*
> *I place my hands so,*

with pollen.
I move my head with pollen.
My feet, my hands, my body
are become pollen,
and my mind, even my voice.
The trail is beautiful.
My lands and my dwelling are beautiful.
Aqalàni, Dinetah.
My spirit wanders across you.
I go to see the Faceless One.
Impervious to pain may I walk.
With beauty all about me may I walk.
It closes in beauty.
I shall not return.
Be still.

Aɴɴ ᴀxᴛᴇʟʟ ᴍᴏʀʀɪs ᴀɴᴅ ʜᴇʀ archaelogist husband Earl told the story of the two Franciscans, Fathers Fintan and Anselm, who traveled in the place of the white reed, *Lu-ka-chu-kai,* in the year 1909. There, south of the Four Corners, in the roadless and wild mountains, they rested one afternoon while their Navajo guide took a walk. Later the guide returned with a large, decorated ceramic water jar. Father Fintan, who knew something of Indian pottery, recognized the uniqueness of the piece and asked where it was from. The guide did not give the location. He did say that it came from an abandoned city of the Anasazi, the Old Ones, a place of many large houses and a high tower—a place where many such jars, some still filled with corn, lay about, as well as blankets, sandals, tools. But he had simply

59

borrowed the jar to show them and must replace it, for one day the owners might return. But where was this place? The Navajo shook his head. He walked off with the pot. After half an hour he was back. Later the priests described the pot to the Morrises, who felt it to be from the Pueblo III period, a high point in southwestern culture. And surely the place would be easy to locate, knowing that it lay within half an hour's walk from that campsite. They searched several times, without success. And Emil W. Haury spent half a summer there in 1927 but was not able to discover the lost city of Lukachukai. There is now a city in Arizona which has taken that name. Rugs are woven there. The story of a lost prehistoric city in those mountains somewhere to the northeast of Canyon de Chelly has since been dismissed as apocryphal.

It was the wind that gave them life. It is the wind that comes out of our mouths now that gives us life. When this ceases to blow we die. In the skin at the tips of our fingers we see the trail of the wind; it shows us where the wind blew when our ancestors were created.

Translated from the Navajo by
Washington Matthews, 1897.

THE BOX HUMMED AND THE OUTLINE occurred, quickly to be filled in and solidified as they watched.

A tall, well-dressed black man of middle years smiled, stepped down and moved forward.

"Good to have you here," Edwin Tedders said, shaking his hand

and turning toward the others. "This is Charles Fisher, stage magician, mentalist."

He indicated a pale woman whose blue eyes were framed by an ultrafine net of wrinkles, her blond hair drawn back and bound.

"This is Elizabeth Brooke, the artist and writer," he said. "Perhaps you've read—"

"We've met," Fisher said. "How are you, Elizabeth?"

She smiled.

"Fine, for a change. And yourself?"

Her accent was British, her ring was expensive. She rose, crossed to Fisher and embraced him lightly.

"Good to see you again," she said.

"We worked together several years ago," she told Tedders. "I'm glad you could get him."

"So am I," Tedders said. "And this is Mercy Spender. . . ."

Fisher moved to the heavyset woman with puffy features and watery eyes, a red spiderweb design beneath the skin of her nose. She wiped her hand before clasping his. Her eyes darted.

"Mercy . . ."

"Hello."

". . . And this is Alex Mancin. He works for the World Stock Exchange."

Alex was short and plump, with a boyish face beneath graying hair. His eyes were steady, though, and there was a look of depth to them.

"Glad to meet you, Mr. Fisher."

"Call me Charles."

"Glad to meet you, Charles."

". . . And this is James MacKenzie Ironbear, a satellite engineer," Tedders said, moving on.

"Jim."

"Dave."

James Ironbear was of middle height, solidly built, with long black hair, dark eyes and a dark complexion. His hands were large and strong-looking.

61

"We've worked together, too," he said. "How've you been, Charles?"

"Busy. I'll tell you all about it later."

"And this," Tedders gestured toward the large smiling man with narrow pale eyes who stood beside the bar, a drink in one hand, "this is Walter Sands. He plays cards, and things like that."

Fisher raised his eyebrows, then nodded.

"Mr. Sands . . ."

"Mr. Fisher."

". . . And so we are gathered," Tedders said. "Everyone else has reviewed the chips."

"I have, too," Fisher said.

"Well, everyone else has an opinion. Do *you* think you'll be able to detect the approach of the Stragean adept?"

"I'm not sure," Fisher replied, "when it comes to an alien with some sort of training."

"That's what everyone else said. May I offer you a drink?"

"Actually, I'd like some food. I came from a different time zone. Haven't had a chance at dinner yet."

"Surely."

Tedders moved to an intercom and pressed a button, ordered a tray.

"They'll serve it on the second floor," he said. "I suggest we all head upstairs and work things out there. It may be a bit more . . . removed . . . from any action that might occur. So if anyone wants to take a drink along, better get it now."

"I'll have a gin and tonic," Mercy said, rising.

"Wouldn't you rather have a cup of tea?" Elizabeth asked her. "It's very good."

"No. I'd rather have a gin and tonic."

She moved off to the bar and prepared herself a large drink. Elizabeth and Tedders exchanged glances. He shrugged.

"I know what you're thinking," Mercy said, her broad back still toward them, "but you're wrong."

Walter Sands, standing beside her, grinned and then turned away.

Tedders led them from the room, and they followed him up a wide staircase.

It was a front room to which he conducted them. There was a large table at its center, a small piece of equipment on it. A half-dozen comfortable-looking chairs were placed around the table; there was a couch to the left and four smaller tables near the walls, left and right. Three trip-boxes capable of accommodating a pair of people each had been installed along the rear wall. Tedders halted in the doorway and gestured along a cross-corridor.

"Charles," he said, "your bedroom is the second door to the left up that way."

He turned back.

"Make yourselves comfortable, everyone. This is where you will be working. We should have two people in here at all times, listening for the alien while the others rest. You can pair off as you wish and make up your own duty roster. That small unit on the table is an alarm. Slap the button and irritating buzzers will go off all over the place. If you are in your rooms and you hear it, wake up fast and get over here. You can use the trip-boxes to get out if all else fails—"

"Wait a minute," Alex Mancin said. "All of this is of course essential, but you've just raised a question that's been bothering me and probably the others, too. Namely, how far does our responsibility here extend? Say we detect the alien and give the alarm. What then? I'm a telepath, but I can also transmit thoughts to others—even nontelepaths. Perhaps I could broadcast confusing images and downbeat emotions to this creature. Maybe the others can do other things. I don't know. Are we supposed to try?"

"A good point," Walter Sands said. "I can influence the fall of dice. I might be able to affect someone's optic nerves. In fact, I know I can. I could leave a person temporarily blind. Should I try something like that—or do we just leave the defense to the tough guys once the enemy is in sight?"

"We can't ask you to jeopardize your lives," Tedders replied. "On the other hand, it would be a great help if you could manage something along those lines. I'm going to have to leave that part to

63

your discretion. But the more you can do, the better, even if it is only a parting shot."

"Charles and I once combined the force of our thinking to pass a message under very trying circumstances," Elizabeth said. "I wonder what would happen if all of us attempted it and directed the results against the alien?"

"I guess that's for you to work out," Tedders said. "But if you're going to try it, don't just blast away at anything indiscriminately. We may have outside help."

"We will learn quickly to recognize the guards if we haven't already done so," Sands said.

"But you may occasionally pick up the thoughts of someone who is not one of the guards," Tedders stated. "I don't want you trying to fry his frontal lobes just because he seems a little different."

"What do you mean? Who is it?" Mercy inquired. "I think you'd better explain."

"His name is William Blackhorse Singer, and he's a Navajo Indian tracker," Tedders replied. "He's on our side."

"Is that the guy who practically filled that Interstellar zoo out in California?" James Ironbear asked.

"Yes."

"What, specifically, will he be up to?"

"I'm not certain. But he says he's going to help."

They all stared at Tedders.

"Why don't you know?" Fisher said.

"He thinks the alien might be a telepath, too. He doesn't want to risk her learning his plans from us. And he thinks he might be able to block a telepath, at least part of the time."

"How?" Sands asked.

"Something to do with thinking in a primitive fashion. I didn't understand it all."

"The Startracker," Ironbear said. "I read about him when I was a kid."

"He a relative or something?" Fisher asked, moving toward a chair and seating himself.

Ironbear shook his head.

"My father was a Sioux from Montana. He's a Navajo from Arizona or New Mexico. No way. I wonder how you think primitive?"

A man carrying a tray came up the hall. Tedders nodded toward Fisher as he brought it into the room. It was delivered and uncovered. Fisher began his meal. Ironbear seated himself across from him. Elizabeth drew out the chair to Fisher's right, Sands the one to his left. Mancin and Mercy Spender seated themselves with Ironbear.

"Thank you," Mancin said. "We are going to have to discuss this now."

"You will have no objections if I record your discussion?" Tedders said. "For later reference."

Sands smiled and an olive left Fisher's salad and drifted toward his hand.

"If you have a machine capable of recording our deliberations I would be very surprised," Mancin said.

"Oh. In that case, I guess there is no reason for me to remain here. When should I check back with you?"

"In about an hour," Mancin said.

"And could you send up a large pot of coffee and some cups?" Ironbear asked.

"And some tea," Elizabeth said.

"I'll do that."

"Thanks."

Tedders moved toward the door.

Mercy Spender looked at her empty glass, began to say something and changed her mind. Elizabeth sighed. Sands chewed the olive. Ironbear cracked his knuckles. No one spoke.

"**I**T IS SAID THAT YOU PAPAGOS HAVE songs of power which give you control over all things."

"So it is said."

"Is it not true?"

"We have no control over the minerals beneath our land."

"Why is this?"

"We are not Navajos."

"I do not understand."

"The Navajos have a treaty with the government which gives them these rights."

"And you do not?"

"To have a treaty with the government you must first have made war upon it. We never looked ahead to see its benefits and we remained at peace. A treaty beats a song of power."

"You make it sound like a card game."

"The Navajos cheat at cards, too."

• • •

"Coyote, you learned the secret of the floating-water place. You kidnapped the child of Water Monster whom you found there. As a result of your tampering with these forces you have unleashed floods, disasters, upheavals of nature. These have led to death, disorder and madness among the People. Why did you do it?"

"Just for laughs."

• • •

"I understand that Begochidi-woman, Begochidi, Talking-god and Black-god created the game animals, and so they have control over the hunt?"

"Yes. They can help a hunter if they wish."

"But you no longer hunt as much as you used to."

"This is true."

"Then they have less work these days."

"I imagine they find ways to keep busy."

"But, I mean, are these the full parameters of their functions as totemic beings within the context of your present tribal structure?"

"What do you mean?"

"Is that all they do?"

"No. They also revenge their people upon anthropologists who tell lies about us."

. . .

In the center of my house of yellow corn I stand, and I
   say this: I am Black-god who speaks to you.
I come and stand below the north. I say this:
Down from the top of Darkness Mountain which lies before
   me a crystal doe stands up and comes to me.
Hooftip to kneetip, body to face, followed by game of all kinds,
it walks into my hand. When I call to it, when I pray
   for it, it comes to me, followed by game of all kinds.
I am Black-god who speaks to you. I stand below the north.
They come to me out of Darkness Mountain.

Mercy Spender,

born at an illegal distillery in Tennessee,
orphaned at the age of 5,
raised by an eccentrically religious aunt on her mother's side
      & her deputy sheriff husband,
      who was taciturn & mustachioed,
      liked bowling & fishing
      & sang in a barbershop quartet,
along with two older girls

     & a boy who raped her at age 11, Jim,
     now a real estate appraiser,
lost any desire for further education at age 12,
sang in the church choir
& later in a bar called Trixie's,
had a series of tediously similar love affairs,
began drinking heavily at age 19,
discovered the joys of the Spiritualist Church at age 20,
        where her peculiar abilities blossomed
        shortly before her commitment
        to a drying-out sanitorium in South Carolina,
        where she found peace
        in the shelter of the therapeutic community,
spent the following 12 years singing, playing the organ,
giving readings & comfort at the Church
& drinking & returning to the therapeutic community
for peace & shelter & drying out,
& singing & comforting & supporting & reading
& drying out &

                         we understand, sister, rest with us,
                         the same under skin, all

             Alex Mancin,

born in New Bedford,
passed through a number of private schools,
doing well without trying hard,
mastering the complicated computer World Economy game model
     by age 11,

J.D., Yale, M.B.A., Harvard Business School,
passing through three marriages,
doing less well without trying any harder,
     by age 36
father of two sons (twins) & three daughters
     for whom he feels as much affection
     as he has ever felt for anyone,
aware of everyone's opinion about him
     because of his strange sensitivity to thoughts
     & not really caring a bit,
passionately devoted to a kennelful of Italian greyhounds,
     like Frederick the Great, whom he also admires,
     & far more concerned about canine thought-processes
     than those of people,
an absolute master of the money market,
rich as Croesus,
slow to anger & very slow to forgive,
greatly concerned about his appearance & dress,
wondering occasionally whether there is something he is missing,
seeking—every two or three years (unsatisfactorily)—
     for omitted fulfillments
     in orgies of high cultural immersion
     & passing love affairs
     with very young women,
highly intelligent & partially numb

> *a piece of everyone,*
> *none of us complete, brother,*
> *save when together,*
> *like this*

Roger Zelazny

Charles Dickens Fisher,

born in Toronto of a physician father & sociologist mother,
became fascinated by illusion at an early age,
put on magic shows for his sisters, Peg & Beth,
was a good student though not an outstanding one,
read the lives of the great illusionists,
      Houdin, Thurston, Blackstone,
      Dunninger, Houdini, Henning,
learned that he could cast illusions himself
    with no other equipment
    than strong thoughts,
left school & became an entertainer
    against his parents' wishes,
grew famous as an in-person showman
    (his illusions would not televise),
was later approached by the government
    on the basis of an uncanny mentalist act
    he subsequently tried,
has since done considerable security work
both in & out of government,
    never married, always maintaining
    that the life he leads is too demanding
    of his time & energy,
    that he will not change
    & that he will not be unfair
    by subjecting another person
    to confinement in a pigeonhole
    in his schedule,
is actually afraid to commit himself
    too strongly to another human being
    or to give up the emotions
    of audience attention he feeds upon,
possesses the compassion of a full empath,

70

has a few good friends & many acquaintances,
is aware of his deficiencies
    & mocks himself often,
tends to grow maudlin around the holidays,
still dotes on his sisters & their children,
has never been fully reconciled with his parents,
sometimes hates himself for disappointing

> *but here we are*
> *what we are,*
> *& knowing it all,*
> *there is shelter*
> *& pain drains away*

Walter Sands,

left home when he was 14,
    after blinding the stepfather who beat him,
knowing he had the power & could make his way,
big for his age,
won most fights
    (with a little help from the power)
& most games of chance
    (ditto),
seldom held a real job,
    save as a kind of cover,
enlisted in the Perimeter Patrol at age 18—
    the international Coast Guard-like space service—
    for a 4-year hitch

71

because he wanted to see
what was Out There,
was well-liked,
could have become an officer if he'd cared to stay,
didn't, though,
because he'd seen what he'd joined to see
& that was enough,
grew darkly handsome,
avoided close emotional involvements
though he liked people,
singly & in groups,
except once,
married at 28, divorced at 30,
one daughter, now 16, Susannah,
whose picture he carries,
& that was enough,
likes spectator sports, travel & historical novels,
seldom overindulges in anything,
is totally irreligious,
but prides himself
on a personal code involving honor,
which he has only violated 6 or 7 times
and always felt bad about
afterwards,
is normally trustworthy but seldom trusts,
having seen the insides
of too many heads,
suffers, if anything,
from a feeling that life is
& always will be
too secure & bland a thing for him,
which is why he enjoys vicarious risks,
which usually turn into sure things,
leaving him vaguely dissatisfied

this one may prove
more interesting,
fortunate brother,
if not peace
then adrenalin
to you

Elizabeth Brooke,

daughter of Thomas C. Brooke, painter, sculptor,
      & Mary Manning, concert pianist, author,
younger of two daughters,
showed artistic & literary aptitudes in early childhood,
vacationed with her family every summer
      in France, Ireland
      or Luna City,
schooled in Switzerland & Peking,
married Arthur Brooke (first cousin)
      at age 24,
widowed at age 25,
no children,
lost herself in social work
      on Earth & off
      for the following 6 years,
      where her unfolding talent
      was both her joy & her grief,
returned to writing & painting,
      exhibiting extraordinary perceptive powers,

73

    understanding of the human spirit
      & technical abilities,
has enjoyed a liaison with a high-ranking
      MP for the past 6 years,
has always felt partly responsible for Arthur's death
      because of a series
      of bitter confrontations
      following her discovery of his homosexuality

> *we hold you, sister,*
> *against the*
> *unchanging past*
> *in warmth*
> *& full understanding*

James MacKenzie Ironbear,

half Scot, half Oglala Sioux,
born on reservation land,
parents separated early,
raised by his mother in Bloomington, Indiana,
    & Edinburgh, Scotland,
      where she worked for the universities'
      custodial staffs,
displayed high mechanical aptitudes
    & telepathic abilities
      before age 5,
seldom visited relatives on his father's side,
first-class baseball & soccer player,
could have gone professional

but preferred the engineering
he pursued
on his athletic scholarship,
his best friend an Eskimo boy from Point Barrow,
          they spent their summers together in Alaska
          during their college careers
          as rangers in Gateway to the Arctic
          National Park,
fathered one son, now in his teens
          & living in Anchorage,
later served in Perimeter Patrol
          where his telepathic ability
          came to the attention
          of government authorities,
was recruited for occasional work
          of the sort Charles Fisher
          did for them,
          which is where he met Fisher,
          becoming friends with him,
has since fulfilled 5 separate
          one-year contracts in space engineering,
          working half of the year in orbit,
is on leave of absence from his sixth,
          pending divorce from Fisher's sister, Peg,
          who works for the same company
          & resides in the great tube
          of Port O'Neill
          with their daughter Pamela,
attended his father's funeral this past summer
          & was surprised to find himself deeply saddened
          that he had never known the man,
had suddenly decided to chuck everything
          & study music,
          an enterprise commenced
          when he sobered up a month later

& followed diligently
until this call came in,
finding himself thinking more & more
of his shrunken father,
lying there in a beaded leather jacket,
& of the son
he has not seen in years

come close, brother,
where we who
are greater than one
hold greater understanding,
absorb more hurt

"**I**T IS GOOD THAT YOU WISH TO WALK
in beauty, with beauty all around you, my son. But a hunter should
not speak prayers from the Blessingway during the hunt, for they all
have the life blessing at the end and you require a prayer of death.
To Talking-god must you speak, and to Black-god: Aya-na-ya-ya!
Eh-eh-eh! Here is the time of the cutting of the throat! Na-eh-ya-ya!
It happens in a holy place, the cutting of the throat! Ay-ah, na-ya-
ya! The cutting of the throat is happening now in a holy place! Na-
ya-ya! It is the time of the cutting of the throat! Ya-eh-ni-ya!
    "It is not always life that must be blessed."

76

N IGHT. HE STANDS BEFORE THE FORCE
wall. He watches the rock unfold itself.

There are clouds in your mind, hunter.

There are many things in my mind, Cat.

You have come. Have we a bargain?

Do as I asked you and I will do as you asked me.

We have a bargain. Release me.

It will take a minute or so.

The form rose to become a white pillar, the single, faceted eye
drifting upward along it. Billy Singer moved to the area where the
controls were housed. He opened the case and lowered the potential
of the field.

The base of the pillar split and forelimbs disassociated themselves
from the main mass higher up. A bulbous protruberance grew at the
top, the eye coming to rest at its center. The forked segments became
leglike. A tightening at the middle was suddenly a narrow waist. The
head elongated, growing vaguely lupine. The shoulders widened, the
arms and legs thickened. Excess mass was shifted behind, becoming
a broad tail. The manlike thing was tall, over two meters, and it
darkened as it moved forward, exhibiting a grace which suggested
earlier rehearsal of the form.

Silent for all of its bulk, it removed itself from the enclosure and
went to stand before the man.

*I suggest you restore the force screen. That way it could be several
days before they notice my absence. I have accustomed them to such a
situation by assuming the appearance of portions of the habitat for
days at a time.*

I had already thought of that, Billy replied. *But first I wanted to
watch you change.*

You were impressed?

Yes. You do it quickly, he said in his mind, turning the field on again. *Come. I'll take you to a trip-box now. You will have to charge it to my number without my card—which will require a confirmation by me from the other end, since I'll have to pass through first and—*

I know how they work. I have had little but the thoughts of your fellows to fill me for a long while.

Come, then.

Billy turned away and moved across the hall.

You show me your back. Do you not fear that I will leap upon you and rend you? Or is your action calculated?

I feel you wish to encounter the Stragean. Kill me now and the opportunity will be lost to you.

A shadow as silent as himself—somewhat more manlike than moments earlier, and hence more alien—came abreast of him to the left. It matched his pace, the movements of his arms, all of his rhythms. He could feel its power as they glided through the hall. Inhabitants of the enclosures they passed shifted uneasily, whether in sleep or full wakefulness. Billy felt a touch of amusement in the alien mind at his side—and then a broadcast *Farewell!* which roused the creatures to frantic activity.

He led the way outside, where he breathed deeply of the night air. The creature at his side dropped to all fours, then moved away, sliding into and out of shadows from unsuspected directions as they advanced.

From somewhere up ahead, a dog began to bark—a sound terminated in midnote to the accompaniment of a brief thrashing noise. Billy did not change his pace, knowing by senses other than sight that Cat was with him all the way to the trip-box.

All right, he said. *I'll key the thing. I will go through to a small public box a few miles from the place we will be guarding. If there is any reason at that end for you not to come through, I will use the communicator. Otherwise, be ready to follow me.*

A piece of shadow came loose nearby and drifted toward him. It was even more manlike in proportion now and had fabricated what

78

could have been a long black cloak out of its own substance. The massive, faceted eye was deeply submerged within its head and masked by connective tissues in such a fashion as to give the impression of a pair of glittering, normally placed eyes.

On second thought, Billy said when he looked at him, *I believe you could pass even if there is someone there.*

I see the direction of your thoughts, if dimly. I will formulate something to resemble darkened glasses and muster something nearer to human skin-coloration. Why are your thoughts so clouded?

I am practicing to deceive our enemy, Billy replied, entering the box. *I will see you soon.*

Yes. I cannot be lost so easily, tracker.

He watched Billy manipulate the controls and fade within the enclosure. Then he entered there himself. Extending what had become his right hand, he covered the slot where Billy had briefly inserted his credit slip. A portion of that appendage flowed into the opening and explored there for a time. When the call came through, he withdrew it and allowed himself to be transported.

Strange, a singing in his mind. Was there something in the places between the places, to sing so of frost and iron, fire and darkness? In a moment, it and its memory were gone.

> *Between the worlds walking.*
> *Between the worlds walking.*
> *Between the worlds walking.*
> *Between the worlds walking.*
> *There is something*
> *before me, behind me,*
> *to right and to left,*
> *above and below.*
> *What, on all sides,*
> *is it?*

A LEX MANCIN HIT THE BUTTON WHEN
he detected the presence, a moment before Walter Sands's hand
jerked in the same direction. Buzzing sounds filled the house and
light flooded the lawns about it.

Yes

Mercy Spender joined them a moment later, sitting up
in her bed

I can feel them

Them?

joined Fisher, putting down his book

There is only one

A man

Ironbear joined, from sleep

moving strangely
nearby
Singer
no doubt

No man

joined Elizabeth, chasing dreams of dolphins

Something else
thing filled with hate
flowing

Together then

Sands joined

let us explore this

Yes

together we move

There is a man

fading now

and something else
alien thing

80

> *aware of us*
>   *fading also*
> *with the man*
>   *the thing is not the thing*
>   *we seek*
> *it hunts*
> *with the man*
>   *our common enemy*
> *retreating now*
>   *it sensed us*
>   *we know its signature*
>   *Shall we follow?*
>   *turn off the alarm*
>   *the guards come*
>   *we must report*
>   *I will follow*
>   went Mercy, departing
>   *the beast*
>   *if I can*
>   *and I the man*
>   moved Ironbear away
>   *though the trail*
>   *I fear*
>   *is covered now*
>   *apart break we then*
>   *we will report*
>   Mancin and Sands, dividing

The following day, within a stand of trees about forty meters from the road, Billy Singer sat beside an icy stream, his back against a large, warm rock. He was eating a roast beef sandwich, watching the flight of birds, listening to the wind and observing the behavior of a small squirrel in the lower branches of a tree upstream, to his right.

Something hunts nearby, the other told him.

Yes, I know, he answered in thought.

Something large.
I know that, too.
It comes this way.
Yes. What is it?
I cannot tell. Come inside. We will observe.

Billy rose silently to his feet. The rock split down the middle vertically and opened like an upended clam. Even as he watched, the cavity within grew large, outside surfaces swelling proportionately. He entered, and it closed about him.

Darkness, pierced by a few small holes, forward . . .

He placed his eye against one. He was facing the stream. For a time, nothing happened. Several more apertures appeared before him, but the section he regarded remained unchanged.

Then he heard the splashing sounds. Something was approaching from beyond the shrub-lined bend. His stream of consciousness fell still. His was now the passive eye of the hunter, discerning everything before it without reflection. His breathing slowed even further. Time ceased to exist. Now . . .

First, a shadow. Then, slowly, the branched head appeared from beyond the bend. A deer, browsing along the stream bed . . .

Yet . . .

It moved again, forward, the rest of its body coming into view. There was something wrong with the way that it moved and held its head. The legs did not bend in quite the proper fashion. And the shape of the head was unusual. The cranium rose too high above the eyes. . . .

Deerlike . . . Yes. A good approximation, perhaps, for someone who had only studied tridees of the creature. No doubt close enough to deceive any casual observer. But to Billy it could only be deerlike. He wondered whether Cat realized this, too.

. . . *Yes* drifted through his mind.

Immediately, the creature before them froze, one less-than-delicate forelimb raised. Then the head turned, moving through unnatural angles to survey everything at hand.

Moments later, the creature exploded into movement, the entire body twisting, elongating, legs thickening, shortening, bunching.

And then it sprang off, back in the direction from which it had come.

Even as this occurred his shelter opened, regurgitating him with some force, and by the time Billy had regained his footing Cat was in the process of transformation back into the form of the hunting beast.

Not waiting for the metamorphosis to run its course, Billy ran in the direction the creature had taken, splashing into the stream and following it beyond the bend.

His eyes scanned both banks, but he discerned no signs that it had departed the water at either hand. He splashed onward, over gravel, sand and slick rocks, continuing his surveillance.

For a long while, he followed the twisting, watery route. But he heard no further sounds from ahead, nor could he detect any evidence of the creature's having departed the stream. He halted at a rocky shingle to study it with extra care. As he did, he heard sounds of approach from the rear.

Farther ahead! Farther ahead! Cat told him. *I've touched her mind. It slips away. But she betrays herself occasionally.*

He turned and raced ahead. Cat bounded past him.

Something is happening. She is shifting again. She is up high somewhere now. She— Lost her . . .

Billy continued his advance along the watery way. Cat hurried on ahead and was lost moments later beyond the screening brush. After perhaps five minutes, Billy found what he had been seeking.

There was sign of something having left the water. He followed it up and to the right. The first clear print he located, however, was a peculiar, triple-pronged thing. But it was sufficiently large, and its depth in soil of that consistency was indication of the sort of mass that he knew he followed. The spoor led him off toward higher ground, and the next clear print he came upon showed a further alteration of shape.

And he came across the even fresher signs of Cat, still on the trail. Cat's tracks were far apart and deeply sunk.

83

The way remained clear and he was able to increase his pace. Moving at a very fast walk, uphill, down, then up again, he felt the old tingling sensation as the quarry's track vanished, to reappear forty feet away, lighter, slightly reshaped, and then to vanish again. Pictures occurred within his mind, his natural ability to form them enhanced by his alien experiences. He read the sign correctly, and he looked upward in time to see a vast, dark shape glide overhead, moving in a southwesterly direction. And even as he hurried to climb a tree, he knew that, for the moment, the quarry had won.

He achieved a suitable vantage only in time to see the dark thing slip out of sight beyond a distant tree-line.

. . . How clever! Cat's thought came to him. *I wonder whether I could do that?*

At least it was not headed toward the mansion, Billy said. *We had best return to our post, though.*

You go, Cat replied. *I am going to try following her. I will meet you there later.*

Very well.

Before he climbed down he noted through an opening in the leaves an area above him that had been blackened and broken. It had not been a recent thing, but he shuddered at one of the old superstitions reaching out for him at this time. Of all the trees present, he had chosen a lightning-struck one to climb. Thing of ill-fortune . . . He sang a section from the Blessingway as he descended. The part of him which did not fear the lightning was standing far away now, clad in different garments.

How much had the Stragean learned of what it was that pursued her? Cat, keep your presence of mind, he thought. Do not betray yourself in the fury of the hunt. Or are your instincts proof even against one such as you follow?

He reached the ground and turned back. What would Nayenezgani have done?

He did not know.

Sun come down the sky from straight to slant again drifting waterwards gaze of Billy's mind with it to flow time undoing knots touch of cloud to dark the sky as hand with knowledge of own scoops among sands at shore blue gray white yellow no red no real black no matter bird above hunkered form of man on tree limb singing leaves shifting in wind fish in water decomposable soda bottle decomposing across the riverrun.

Without thought, dipping his hands. A pinch of sand in the right palm, beneath the second finger. Hand turning. A trickle from the index finger, thumb regulating its flow. Movement. The hand has not forgotten. The lines. The angles. Blue and white and yellow here. Náa-tse-elit, the Rainbow *yei* taking form, guarding the south, the west and the north, open to the east. Within, the body of Thunder, *Ikne'etso,* a bat guardian above his head, messenger of the Night, east, an arrow, *ash-tin,* west. A great power here. One of the unpredictable, dangerous gods. Holder of lightning. Humming to himself, pieces of the Mountain Chant, finishing, staring, Billy. For a long time, staring.

Slowly, the awareness. A peculiar thing to have done. Consciously or automatically. Of all things to call upon, why Thunder? For that matter, why call at all? However things fell out, he would be the loser. Yet he reached forward to touch *ikne'eka'a,* the lightning, to transfer the medicine and the power, since it was there before him.

And now . . . A day sandpainting must be erased before the sun sets. With a sacred feather staff it is to be erased. He recalled the black feather in the *tchah* and withdrew it and used it to this end, casting the sand away into the water.

85

Roger Zelazny

Sun go down the sky rolling west
Time undoing knots
No real color
Ikne'etso *and* Náa-tse-elit *into the riverrun*

recirculation

SINGING NOW. BILLY BLACKHORSE
Singer. At the corner of the estate. Night. Spring constellations
filling the heavens. Coyote cries faded.

They had located her again at evening, circling, circling at a great
distance, probing, carefully advancing. They had waited.

She had come, slowly, in many guises. Skimming, burrowing,
flowing. They had waited. And when the night was complete, she
came on.

One moment Cat had been at his back, dark stony buttress to the
wall itself. Then a huge shape had drifted overhead, blotting stars.
The buttress had flowed upward, coalescing into a nightmare outline
atop the wall. Then a second dark shape rode the air currents,
sought altitude, circled, slid through the night toward the house.

He was never certain at what point the encounter occurred and
the struggle commenced, whether it was in the air, on the ground,
outside the house or within. But he heard a series of unearthly cries
at about the same time that the lights came on all over the grounds.
He remained unmoving in his shadowy corner, listening to the
various sounds which ensued—crashes, buzzes, the breaking of glass,
several small explosions. These continued for nearly a minute before
all of the lights went out.

And he waited. He could think of nothing for which he might

86

hope. He remembered things, and he sang the song softly.

Then the silence came again. He regarded the sky as the moment stretched. His words neither hurried nor slowed in their passage across the night.

A single loud crash occurred, followed by some lesser sounds. Then again the silence. A small light appeared behind a pair of upstairs windows.

Cat?

A large form emerged from the front of the house, dropped to all fours, moved slowly away. Nothing moved to interfere with it. The night remained quiet. Billy followed its progress with his eyes. He knew that it was time for the song to end. He carried a knife and a computer-targeting laser sidearm. If this were the Stragean, he felt obliged to attempt her destruction. He drew the weapon and placed his thumb on the set stud.

This is how you keep your promise, hunter?

Cat!

Yes. She fought well but she is dead. I have broken her. Shall we see now whether you can activate the weapon before I can reach you? Ten meters separate us and I am ready to spring. The weapon is faster than I am, but is your thumb? I will know the moment that you decide to move it. Go ahead. Any time now . . .

No.

Billy tossed the weapon into the shrubbery to his right.

I did not know which of you it was moving this way.

He detected a sense of puzzlement, underlined by a touch of pain.

You were injured?

It is nothing.

Both remained unmoving.

Finally, *As you said, any time now,* Billy stated.

You offer me no contest.

No.

Why not? You are a predator, like me.

We have a bargain.

What is that when it is your life? I expected resistance.

87

Cat detected something like puzzlement.

I made you a promise.

But I took it to mean that you would await my attack here and defend yourself when the time came.

I am sorry. That was not my understanding. But now I have no intention of giving you a token fight. You require my life. Take it.

Cat began a slow advance, his form dropping nearer and nearer to the ground. When he raised his head once more it bore an enormous, horned, fanged, semihuman face—a bestial parody of Billy's own. Suddenly then, Cat reared, to raise that head fully eight feet above the ground. He glared down.

Billy shuddered, but he held his place.

You are taking much of the pleasure from it, hunter.

Billy shrugged.

That cannot be helped.

Cat began to unfurl great membranous wings behind him. After a time, he folded them about himself and became a still, dark pillar.

Finally, *If you can make it over the wall before I reach you,* Cat said, *I will let you go.*

Billy did not move.

No, he said. *I know that I could not do it. I will not make the attempt just to provide you with sport.*

The pillar blossomed, an exotic flower opening to reveal a tigerlike head. It swayed toward him.

You pursued me for over a week, Cat said at last. *While I have dreamed of your death, I have dreamed, too, of hunting you. Your death alone should be sufficient, but I do not want it to be over with in an instant. It troubles me, too, that I do not know whether this desire springs from that which I know best—the hunt—or whether my long mental association with your own kind has taught me somewhat of the joys of prolonging an enemy's agony.*

Both are sufficiently primitive, Billy replied. *I wouldn't worry about it.*

I do not. But I desire the hunt, and I see now that only one thing will make you give it to me.

And what is that?

Your life. A chance to regain it.

Billy laughed.

I have already resigned myself to dying. Do you believe yourself the only misfit alien on this world, Cat? My people—my real people—are also dead. All of them. The world in which I now find myself is a strange place. The Dineh are not as I once knew them. Your offer only brought my condition into full focus. And I have prepared myself for this.

Cat drew back.

Years ago, he said, *I saw in your mind a great pride in your people's ability to adapt. Now you say that it is gone from you. I say this means that you have become a coward, seeing death as the easy way out.*

Billy stiffened.

That is not true!

Look within yourself. I have but given you an excuse to resign.

No!

Then fight me, Billy. Pit your skills against me one more time.

I—

You are afraid now, where you were not before. You are afraid to live.

That is not so.

Would you say it four times, man of the People?

Damn you, Cat! I was ready, ready for you! But you are not satisfied with just my life. You wish to fill me with uncertainty before you kill me!

If that is what it takes, yes. I see now that there would be small pleasure in slaying you like some brainless piece of meat that waits to be slaughtered. My full revenge requires the joy of the hunt. So I will make you an offer, and I will have you know that my promise will be as good as yours, Billy Singer—for I cannot let you beat me even in that thing. Go. Flee. Cover your trail, tracker. I will give you what I judge to be an hour—and I am fairly good at estimating time—and then I will pursue you. You tracked me for nearly eight days. Let us call it a week.

*Keep alive for that long and I will renounce my claim upon your life.
We will go our ways, free of one another.*

And what will be the rules? Billy asked.

*Rules? If you can kill me before I kill you, by all means do so. In
any manner. Go anywhere that you wish by any means that you choose.
Anything is fair. There are no rules in the hunt. Live out the week and
you will be rid of me. You will not make it, though.*

Who can say?

What is your answer?

Billy turned, took several quick steps and leaped, catching hold of
the top edge of the wall. He drew himself up in a single, swinging
motion.

Start counting, he said, as he dropped down onto the other side
and broke into a run.

Cat's laughter followed him for over a minute.

PART II

Things that flee and things that pursue
have their seasons.
Each of us hunts
and each of us is hunted.
We are all of us prey;
we are all predators.
Knowing this, the careful hunter
is wary. The prey, too, learns boldness
beyond its normal reach.
And then there is luck,
and then the gods.
The hunt is always uncertain.

We skinned the wolf
and in the morning
a human hide hung there.
At night, it became again
the pelt of a wolf.

There is no certainty,
there is no law
in the hunt.

Talking-god be with me.
Black-god be with me.
Luck and boldness
be with me, too.

〉&⇒*The First Day*   WITHOUT SLOWING, HE

illuminated the dial of his watch and checked the time. An hour. He smiled, because it seemed that Cat had overlooked the obvious. He could get far in that time, and all was fair. . . .

He maintained the steady pace which he could keep up for most of a day. To give in to fears and sprint now would be to leave himself exhausted in the face of possibly necessary exertions later.

The wind whipped by him, and deeper patches of shadows took on an ominous character, hiding eyes, fangs, movement. . . .

Dead. The Stragean was dead. A being able to cause fear in the highest circles. Dead. And Cat had slain her. Soon Cat would be bounding along, coming this same way. Cat's enormous, faceted eye could, he believed, see into the infrared, distinguish polarized light. He was still not certain as to all of the senses Cat possessed. He could see Cat now, like a giant *chindi*, not even slowing as he followed the trail.

Beads of perspiration formed on Billy's brow. A part of him saw the beast's powers from a completely rational standpoint. He had fought Cat before when Cat was much more naive. But Cat had had fifty years in which to become sophisticated in the ways of this world. Cat suddenly became phantomlike at another level, no longer the beast that had been, but something returning, as from the north. . . .

He fought back a renewed desire to increase his pace. There was ample time, he told himself, a sufficiency in which to make good his getaway. And why should there be fear? Bare minutes ago he had been ready to die. Now at least there was a chance. He strove to contain himself within the present instant. The past was gone. He had some say in the making of the future, but this was contingent upon his behavior now. It was going to be all right. Long before the hour had run out, he would be totally safe. It was only a matter of minutes, really. . . .

He jogged on, his mind fixed upon his goal. At last it came into sight, the trip-box station which would place him beyond Cat's reach in the barest twinkling. He saw the lights of the small building at the crossroads beyond the field he was now entering. Something about it, though . . .

As he moved nearer, he realized that the front window of the place was broken. He slowed his approach. He could see no one about.

He halted and looked inside. There were three units, lined against the far wall. All of them were wrecked. It was as if a piece of runaway heavy equipment had passed through, snapping or twisting the gleaming standards, upsetting the control units. The power banks, he noted, were untouched.

Cat . . .

That last time Cat had gone out, ranging far to scout the area . . . Cat had foreseen a possible escape on his part with flight in this direction, had acted to remedy this means of retreat.

He looked about. The damage should have registered itself at the area control center. But the hour was late. No telling when a repair crew might be by.

A map. There would be a line map inside for the area. He moved to the doorway and entered.

Yes. On the wall to his right. He studied the disposition of the red dots representing boxes in the area, located his own position, looked for the next several.

Four miles to the nearest one.

Would Cat know its location? Would Cat have bothered to look at this thing on the wall, realizing it was a map? And even if this were the case, would Cat have gone to the trouble to wreck another? True, he might have wanted to cover all bets. . . .

But no. Cat's surprise at his failure to flee had seemed genuine. Cat had expected him to run. While it might be possible for him to elude the beast and make it this far, it seemed unlikely that he could reach the next one under these circumstances. So even if Cat did know about it, chances were that the next box remained unmolested.

Still, a map and the land itself were two different things. He was not exactly certain as to the disposition of that next red dot. Even with the grace period, he could be cutting things short.

He departed the wrecked station, took his bearings and re-commenced his steady stride, cutting through a skeleton-limbed orchard that rattled about him as he passed. A rabbit sprang from behind a clump of grasses to veer across his path and vanish into the shadows to the left. The grasses were damp, and soon the lower portions of his trousers were soaked through. Somewhere a dog began barking. He suddenly felt as if he were being watched, from no particular direction. Again the fleeting shadows writhed images.

For a moment, he wondered what time it was, and then the desire to know this thing fell away. Abruptly, he found that he was happy. A part of his mind was almost cheering for Cat, hoping that even now the beast was on his trail. Let it be close. Let it be very close and clean, he felt. Or else what the joy in such a context? This was the most alive he had felt himself in years. There was a new song inside him now, accompanied by his drumbeat footfalls.

He did not try to analyze the shifting of his mood. The clutter of circumstance was far too dense for introspection, even had he felt so inclined. For the moment, it was sufficient to ride with the beat of his flight.

There were times when he felt certain that Cat was right at his back, and it did not seem to matter. Other times, he felt that he had already won, that he had far outdistanced his pursuer, that there was no chance of his ever being overtaken. All of his senses now seemed touched with an unusual acuity—the tiniest night movement was instantly identified, from the faintest rasp, thump or crackling; shadowy forms grew far more distinct, and even odors took on a new significance. It had all been this way once, yes, long ago. . . .

It was before everything that the world had been this way, that he had been this way. Running. Into the east. Vision as yet unclouded by veils life was later to drop upon him. He had been eight or nine years old before he had learned to speak English. . . .

But after all of this, he wondered, what traces really remained of his shift from a near-neolithic to a high-tech society? He had lived more years under the latter than under the former, if these things were to be measured solely in years. The shift had been made successfully, and both ends of his personal spectrum were available to him.

But it was the primitive which ruled as he ran. Yes. And this part preferred the day to the night. Yet the joy remained. It was not that there was an absence of fear. Instead, the fear was contributing something to that peculiar species of elation which had risen within him.

As he pounded along, he wondered what the situation was back at the mansion. What had Walford, Tedders, the defenders and the Strageans made of that sudden attack followed by the death of the adept—with no explanation as to what had occurred? Naturally they would suspect his part in it, but they must be puzzled by his absence. Even now they must be trying to reach him—though this time he was not even wearing the paging unit.

Would they ever learn? He wondered for the first time what Cat might do later—if things were all over and he, Billy Singer, had walked into the north. Would Cat retire to some wilderness area and spend his days passing as some garden variety predator? It seemed possible, but he could not be certain. He could not tell whether Cat's hatred was focused upon him solely or whether he might hold all of humanity responsible for his captivity. Images moved within Billy's mind—crouching in a cage day after day, year after year, being stared at by passing knots of people. If their situations had been reversed, he felt that he would hate all mankind.

A sense of irritation began to grow. Why shouldn't Cat consider him a sacrificial lamb and let it go at that?

He shook his head. No real reason for assuming that Cat would run amok later. He had given no such indication. What was he doing thinking these thoughts, anyway? Looking for trouble? It was him that Cat wanted, not him plus everybody else. And after he had gotten him, it would all be over with. . . .

Sacrificial lamb . . . He thought again of the sheep he had herded as a boy. Long, slow days under skies hot and cool, big skies . . . Lying on a hillside. Whittling. Singing. Foot-races with other children. His first tumble with that girl from over the ridge. What was her name? And later with her sister. Hard breasts under his hands. The sheep about them unconcerned. Clouds like sheep on the horizon. Sheep. Lamb of God. Dora in the sky with turquoise. Running . . .

Cat. Running. How will you track me, Cat? Do you follow the same signs I would? Or does your alien eye trace different marks of passage? Either way, there is no time to mask this trail. Escape first. Hide afterwards. Speed now is all. Speed, opportunity. Chance. How near might you be, anyway? Or are you still waiting for the time to run?

Turquoise in the sky with Dora to the drumbeat footbeat here below. On the hillside, far ahead, lights. Night air comes in, goes out again. Stride is steady. Veer left, beyond the death-shaped boulder. Up then. Cat come. Into the black bag. Full entropy is all. But first.

Minutes melting, one to the other. In the distance, the hum of a super battery-powered vehicle above the cleared trail which had once been a roadway, lights raking tree trunks. Heading for the station perhaps. Ay-ah! We live. Unless Cat even now . . .

Drawing nearer, he slowed. This would be the place for an ambush. Why not check the time? Because Cat might have lied to gain this much of a chase. Once through the box and the beast would be baffled. Wouldn't he?

Walking now, he examined a new proposition. What had Cat said about understanding the boxes?

No. Even if he could black-fare his way, he would not know where to go. . . .

Cat is a telepath.

But of what sort? He had estimated Cat's ability as a hunting/locator thing, refined, to be sure, during his long confinement, but basically quarry-intensive, at about a quarter of a mile. Still, there were human telepaths he knew of who could send and receive around the world and through outer space. Yet, again, such sophisticated ones he felt he could block to some extent by slipping back to boyhood thought patterns. But Cat, too, was primitive. It might not serve to hide him from the beast. In which case.

The devil with you, Cat!—on all fours now, carefully clearing the way before him of anything which might give rise to the slightest sound, his jewelry wrapped in a handkerchief and stuffed into his pocket, hands moving deftly, knees and toes advancing into the cleared area in total silence. *Find me if you can. Fight me if you do.*

No response. And nothing between here and there that he could conceive of as a transformation of his adversary. The car drew up before the building and hovered. No one departed it.

He was on his feet and sprinting across the final meters of the field, through a fringe of trees, over the road-bed trail. A glimpse through the station window: the units were intact.

Almost laughing, he thrust the door open and crossed the threshold. Empty. Safe. Breathe easily. He straightened from his half-crouch, removed his hand from the handle of his knife. Closed the door. All right. Five paces to liberty.

The unit to his far left was humming in preparation for a transfer.

Curious, he watched it. It was an odd hour and a fairly isolated station; he wondered who might be coming through. Shortly, the outline began to form. It was that of a woman, somewhat stocky, with close-cropped brown hair. She wore a dark suit and carried a recording unit bearing the insignia of a major news service in her left hand. Her eyes fixed upon him as she took on solidity.

"Hello," she said, studying his garb.

She stepped out of the unit.

"Hello."

"Coming or going?" she said.

"Just going. I only waited to see if you were someone I knew."

"You're a real Indian, aren't you? Not just someone dressed that way."

"I am. If you called ahead for a car I just saw one pull up out front."

"I did. That must be it." She started forward, then hesitated. "Do you live in this area?" she asked him.

"No. Just visiting."

He moved toward the nearest unit.

"Just a second," she said. "I've come here on a story, or what could be a story. Maybe you'd know something about it."

He forced himself to smile as he took another step.

"I doubt that. Haven't seen anything newsworthy."

"Well," she persisted, "there have been reports of peculiar security measures being taken at the Walford place for some time now. Then suddenly this evening there was apparently a power failure and some disturbance. Now they've gone completely incommunicado. Would you know anything about this?"

He shook his head, moved forward and stepped into the unit.

She followed him and took hold of his arm just as he inserted his strip into the slot, effectively blocking his transit.

"Wait. There's more," she said. "Then we learned that the trip-boxes nearest to the place had been damaged. Are you aware that the next station to the east is out of order?"

"Could it be a part of that power failure?"

"No, no. They have their own power packs—the same as Walford's place, for that matter."

He shrugged, hoping her hand would slip away.

"I'm afraid I don't know anything about it. Listen, I'm in a hurry—"

"You haven't seen or heard of anything unusual in this area?"

He noted that her recorder was switched on.

"No," he said. "I've got to be going now—"

"It's just a feeling," she said, "but I think you know something about this."

"Lady," he said, "your car is waiting. Go and see for yourself like a good reporter. I wouldn't hang around here, though."

"Why not?"

"Maybe something will happen to this one, too."

"Why should it?"

"How should I know? But if there's something dangerous going on, you want to be in its path?"

She smiled for the first time.

"If there's a story in it, yes."

He pushed coordinates.

"Good luck."

"Not yet," she said, still holding his arm. "Have you been by that way at all?"

"Get out of here," he told her, "in the car, or by one of the other booths. Hurry! This place isn't safe. Don't hang around."

"I'll be damned if I'll let you go now!" she said, reaching toward a penlike device clipped behind her lapel.

"Sorry," he said, and he jerked his arm free and pushed her backward. "Do what I said!" he cried. "Get out!" and the fading began.

When he stepped from a unit in London's Victoria Station, pocketing his strip, he had to restrain himself from running. He drew the back of his hand across his brow and it came away wet.

He headed for the nearest exit. The light of a gray morning shone through it. He was arrested momentarily by the smell of food from a twenty-four-hour diner. Too near, he decided, and he moved on outside.

He passed a line of sightseeing hover-vehicles, another of taxis, their operators nowhere in sight. He continued along the way for a time, turned at random in a vaguely northward direction and left the sidewalk. He followed a footpath among trees leading down what had once been a wide thoroughfare. There were fewer streets now than there had been a hundred or even fifty years before, on the occasions of earlier visits he had made. Some main arteries were kept cropped for freighters and the occasional personal hovercraft, some had become malls, some had simply deteriorated, most had become inner-city wilderness areas, or parks, as he used to call them.

He followed the twisting ways for about half an hour, putting a good distance between himself and the station, as the day continued to lighten about him. Muffled by the trees, the sounds of the awakening city grew. He bore to his right, moving into the fringe area.

Above, beyond the walkway, he scanned the faces of opened and opening establishments. Farther ahead, beyond an archway, off a courtyard, he glimpsed a café's sign. He mounted a stair to the walk and headed in that direction. He was, he judged, somewhere near Piccadilly Circus.

Right at the archway, he froze, overwhelmed by a recurrence of the feeling that he was being observed. He looked about. There were a number of people on the walk and in the courtyard, several of them as distinctively dressed as himself for different parts of the world, but none of them seemed to be paying him particular heed, and none seemed large enough to represent the total mass of his adversary.

Of course, it could be something behind him in the woods. . . .

He did not feel like discarding any sort of warning, even a premonition. So he began walking again, passing the archway. In an alcove near the corner ahead, he could see a trip-box. Giving in to nervousness might be a sign of weakness as well as caution, but there

101

was also much to be said for holding onto as much peace of mind as possible when one was running. He quickened his pace.

As he advanced, he saw that the alcove also contained a police callbox. A jerking of its alarm handle should result in the in-tripping of a bobby within seconds, a setup similar to that in use almost everywhere these days. Not that he could see this as helping him very much if he suddenly discovered Cat at his back. A delaying action, at best. And he would probably be condemning the cop to death by calling him. He moved a little more rapidly.

He saw the head of a coyote—no, it was a small dog—appear around the corner of the alcove, looking in his direction. His sense of urgency grew. He fought but could not resist a desire to look back.

When he did, he felt a sudden wave of dizziness. A large man wearing a black cloak and glasses was just emerging from among the trees. Billy broke into a run.

He located and withdrew his credit strip as he raced ahead. He turned it to the proper position for immediate insertion into the machine's slot. A wave of fear washed over him, turning quickly to despair. He was suddenly certain that he could not make it in time. He felt a powerful impulse to halt and wait for his pursuer.

Instead, he plunged into the box, thrust the strip into the slot and rapped out a set of coordinates. Turning then, he saw that the man had dropped to all fours and was racing toward him, changing shape as he came. Someone screamed. Overhead, a dirigible was passing. The entire tableau grew two-dimensional and began to fade. Good-bye, Piccadilly. . . .

Run, hunter, he heard faintly amid his thoughts. *The next time . . .*

He stood in a booth at Victoria Station, shaking. But now it was reaction rather than fear. The fear, the despair, the certainty of doom had vanished at the instant of transport. It was then he realized that Cat must have been projecting these feelings onto him, a slightly more sophisticated version of his old prey-paralysis trick—a thing he had several times felt in its more blatant form years ago. He was startled at the extent to which Cat had developed it since then.

He keyed a chart onto the directory screen and took a new set of coordinates from it. His pursuer might have caught Victoria Station from his thoughts, and—

As he faded, he saw something beginning to take shape two booths up from him, something resembling a tall, cloaked, less-than-human figure still in the process of widening its shoulders and lengthening its forelimbs.

"Damn!"

Yes!

Coming through in Madrid . . . Bright sky through a dirty window. A crowd of commuters. No time . . .

He keyed the directory, hit more coordinates. He looked about as Madrid began to go away. No sign of an incoming torglind metamorph. He began to sigh. Finished sighing at the Gare du Nord boxsection in Paris. He summoned the local directory and tripped again.

Walking. Day brighter yet. From the Tuileries Station. Safe now. No way for Cat to have followed this time.

Passing up the Champs Élysées. Crossing from the fringes of the park over the cyclists' trail and onto the walkway, he smelled the aromas of food from the nearest sidewalk café. He passed several before he settled upon one with a vacant table, close to a trip-box, commanding good views in both directions. He seated himself there and ordered a large breakfast. When he had finished he lingered, drinking countless cups of coffee. Nothing threatening appeared and he felt the flickering beginning of a sense of security. After a time, a feeling of lethargy settled upon him.

Night. It was late morning here, but it was night in the place he had left. He had been a long while without sleep.

He got up and walked again. Should he jump to another city to obscure his trail further? Or had he covered his tracks sufficiently?

He compromised and tripped to the Left Bank. He walked again. He knew that his thinking was foggy. Filled first with the necessities of his flight, his mind was now reduced to slow-motion movement by reaction, by fatigue. It would be easy to obtain a stimulant to restore full alertness, by communication with his medical computer and a request for transmission of a prescription order to a local phar-

103

macist. But he felt relatively safe now, and he would rather rest and restore his natural energies than proceed by artificial means at this stage of affairs. His body might ultimately prove more important than his mind, his feelings and his reflexes surer guides than any elaborate plan. Hadn't he already decided that primitive was best against a dangerous telepath? Sleep now, pay later, if need be.

He located a hotel called the St. Jacques near the University. There were several trip-boxes in the neighborhood and one off the lobby. He took a third-floor room there and stretched out on the bed, fully dressed.

For a long while he stared at the ceiling, unable to sleep. Images of his recent flight came and went. Gradually, however, other images intruded, none of them pieces of recent things. He drifted with them, his breathing slowing, and finally they bore him off.

. . . Watching Dora before the video console, summoning up swarms of equations, fingers moving across the keyboard as his mother's had across the loom, introducing new variables, weaving the fresh patterns that resulted. He did not understand. But it did not matter. Her hair long and blond, her eyes very pale. He had met her on his return from a long expedition, when the Institute had sent him back to school for an update on astrophysical theory and improved navigational techniques. She had taught mathematics there. . . . The equations turn to sandpaintings and finally to skulls, animal as well as human. Dora is smiling. Dimly he remembers that she is dead. Would she still be alive if she had never met him? Probably. But . . . The screen has become a slot machine now, and the skulls keep turning and stopping, coming up different colors. . . . The colors line the walls of the canyon through which he walks. Long bands of strata in the roughness to right and left. Strewn at his feet are the skulls and other bones, some of them gray and gnawed, cracked and weathered, others ivory fresh, some of them inset with turquoise, coral and jet. There comes a sound at his back, but he turns and nothing is there. It comes again, and he turns again, and again there is nothing. The third time it comes, he thinks that he detects a fleeting shadow as he spins around. The fourth time, it is there, waiting. A coyote stands laughing beside a pile of bones. "Come," it says, and it turns away. He follows, and it leads him among the shadows. "Hurry," it says, loping now, and he increases his pace. A long time seems to pass as they move through hidden places. Dark places. Places of forgetfulness. Dora following. Firelight and dancers. Sounds of rattles and drums. Nightclub through a whiskey haze. The dusty surface of Woden IV; the tanklike beasts which dwell there. Bones underfoot, bones all about. Falling, falling . . . Sounds at his back. His shadow preceding him as he pursues the furry tail of the Trickster. "Where are we going?" he calls out. "Out and up, out and up," comes the reply. His shadow is suddenly enveloped by that of a larger one, from something just at his back. "Hurry! Out! Up! Hurry!"

Awakening to urgency: day grown dimmer beyond the window. And what was that sound on the stair?

Out and up? Too strong a thing to ignore. He could almost still hea. ..e coyote beyond the window.

He rose and crossed the room, looked out. There was a fire escape. Had he noticed it on checking in? He did not recall.

He raised the window and stepped outside. He did not question the warning. He still seemed to be moving within the dream. It seemed perfectly reasonable that he continue on the course he had been following. The evening air was cool, trail lights illuminated the way below. That damp, pungent smell on the breeze . . . The Seine?

Up!

He climbed. With some difficulty, he was able to draw himself onto the slanting roof. People were moving along the Rue des Écoles trail, but no one looked upward. He began moving to his right, toes in a rain gutter, hands sliding along slate. The dreamlike quality persisted. He passed chimneys and a dish antenna. He saw a corner ahead. There came a faint, hollow, hammering sound, as of someone pounding on a door, below and to his left. He hurried.

The crashing, splintering sound which followed stirred his imagination but vaguely. There was a booth fairly near now, were he on the ground. . . .

He moved as if following a magic trail, leading toward another fire escape he now had sight of. Even the sounds of pursuit, as a large body passed through his hotel window, ringing upon the metal stair, and then reared to scrabble at the roof's edge, seemed but part of some drama of which he was not even an interested spectator, let alone a principal. He continued to move mechanically, barely aware that his pursuer was addressing him—not with words, but with feelings which he would normally, under the circumstances, have found disquieting.

He glanced back as he took a turn, in time to see the large, oddly shaped figure in black begin to draw itself upward onto the roof. Even when the guttering tore loose beneath its weight and the figure clawed unsuccessfully to gain purchase on the building, he felt no surge of adrenalin. As its downward plunge began, he heard it call: *Today luck is with you. Make the most of it! Tomorrow—*

Its words and movements ceased when it landed in a clump of shrubbery below. And it was only then that he felt as if he were suddenly awakening, realizing that the world actually existed, that his position had been precarious. He drew a deep breath of the night's cold air, swung onto the fire escape and began his descent.

When he reached the ground, the figure was still a dark mass within the *rue*'s trailside growth. It was making small movements and a wheezing noise, but it seemed unable to rise and continue the pursuit.

It was only after he had hurried into the box, summoned forth new coordinates and encoded them that Billy began to wonder.

DISK III

COMPUTER FILES PATENT INFRINGEMENT SUIT

BRG-118, recipient of the 2128 Nobel Prize in Medicine, this morning filed suit in the district court in Los Angeles claiming that J & J Pharmaceuticals

SATELLITE THIEF STRIKES AGAIN

Valuable experimental components were removed from Berga-12 by a person or persons unknown during a power failure now believed to have been induced by

SOLAR REGATTA TO SAIL THURSDAY

REPORTER FOUND BRUTALLY SLAIN

In an out-of-the-way trip-box station in upstate New York, reporter Virginia Kalkoff's mangled

Don't know what I'm gonna do . . .

SPRING STORMS HIT SOUTHWEST

SERIES-12 ARTIFICIAL HEART RECALLED

Apologizing for the inconvenience

IN THE DAYS BEFORE NAYENEZGANI, Old Man Coyote once came upon the Traveling Rock in his journeying about the land. It had spoken to him and he had answered. Amused that a huge pile of stone should possess sentience, he quickly set about mocking it.

First he painted a grotesque face upon its side.

"Old Man Stone, you are frowning," he said.

"I do not like this face you have given me," it replied.

"And you are bald," Coyote said. "I will fix that."

He climbed atop the stone and defecated.

"Brown curly locks suit you well."

"You annoy me, Coyote," it said.

"I will be back in a while to build a fire at your base and cook my dinner," Coyote said, "as soon as I have hunted."

"Perhaps I, too, should hunt," it said.

108

Coyote set off through the woods. He had not gone very far when he heard a rumbling noise behind him. When he looked back he saw that the stone, rolling slowly, had commenced following him.

"Holy shit!" said Coyote, and he began running.

As he ran along, he saw Mountain Lion resting in the shade.

"Mountain Lion!" he called out. "Someone is chasing me. Can you help me, brother?"

Mountain Lion rose, stretched and looked back.

"You've got to be kidding," Mountain Lion said when he saw Traveling Rock. "I've no desire to be a flat cat. Keep going."

Coyote ran on, and later he passed Bear just emerging from his den.

"Hey! Bear, old buddy!" he cried. "I've got someone after me. Will you help me?"

"Sure," said Bear. "There aren't many things I'm afraid of . . .

Then Bear heard the noise of pursuit and looked back and saw Traveling Rock.

". . . But that's one of them," he said. "Sorry."

"What should I do?" Coyote yelled.

"Cultivate philosophy and run like hell," said Bear, returning to his den.

Coyote ran on, down to the plains, and Traveling Rock picked up speed behind him.

At length, Coyote saw Old Buffalo grazing amid long grasses.

"Buffalo! Save me! I'm being chased!" Coyote cried.

Old Buffalo turned his head slowly and regarded the oncoming boulder.

"You can have all the moral support I've got," Buffalo replied. "But I just remembered it's time to move the herd. We've about grazed this area out. See you around, kid. Hey, gang! Let's get our tails across the river!"

Coyote continued to run, gasping now, and finally he came to the place where the hawks were resting.

"Help me, lovely fliers, mighty hunters!" he called. "My enemy is gaining on me!"

109

"Hide in this hollow tree and leave the Rock to us," said the chief of the hawks.

The Hawk Chief gave a signal then and his entire tribe rose into the air, circled once and fell upon the Traveling Rock. With their beaks, they prized away all of its loose covering, and then they went to work along its fracture lines, opening, widening, removing more material. In a short time, the Rock was reduced to a trail of gravel.

"There," said the Hawk Chief to Coyote, "it is over. You can come out now."

Coyote emerged from the tree and regarded the remains of his enemy. Then he laughed.

"It was only a game," he said. "That's all it was. I was never in any real danger. And you dumb birds actually thought I was in trouble. That's funny. That's real funny. No wonder everyone laughs at you. Did you really think I was afraid of that old rock?"

Coyote walked away laughing, and the Hawk Chief gave another signal.

The hawks fell upon the stone chips, gathered them and began reassembling them, like pieces of a gigantic puzzle.

When the Traveling Rock found itself together again, it groaned and then, slowly at first, began rolling, off in the direction Coyote had taken upon his departure. It picked up speed as it moved and soon came in sight of Coyote once more.

"Oh, no!" Coyote cried when he saw it coming.

He began running once again. He came to a downhill slope and began its descent. Traveling Rock picked up speed behind him, narrowed the distance that separated them, rolled over him and crushed him to death.

A circling hawk saw this take place and went back to report it to the others.

"Old Man Coyote has done it again," he said. "He never learns."

✖⇒ *The Second Day*   Night, with mist

banks drifting down rocky slopes, stars toward the center of the sky, moonrise phosphorescence at the edge of things. The floatcar followed the high, craggy trail, winding between rock wall and downward slope, piercing stone shoulders, turning, dipping and rising. Sheep wandered across the way, pausing to browse on spring grasses. There were no lights in the countryside; there was no other traffic. The windshield occasionally misted over, to be cleared by a single, automatic movement of its blade. The only sound above the low buzz of the engine was the occasional urgent note of a gust of wind invading some cranny of the vehicle.

Billy entered a curve bending to his right, a steep rise to his left. He felt more secure with every kilometer that passed. Cat had proved more formidable than he had anticipated when it came to using the trip-boxes and functioning within cities. He was still uncertain as to how the beast had been able to determine his whereabouts with such accuracy. A gimmicking of the boxes he

111

could understand, but knowing where to go to find him . . . It almost smacked of witchcraft, despite the fact that Cat had had a long time in which to plan.

Still, a change of tactics now ought to provide him with the leeway he would need for a total escape. He had tripped back to the Gare du Nord after fleeing the stunned Cat on the Left Bank. From there he had transported himself to Dublin, a city he had visited a number of times during Irish excursions, consulted the directory and tripped to Bantry, from which he had once spent several weeks sailing and fishing. There, in that pleasant, quiet corner of West Cork, he had taken his dinner and known the beginning of this small security he felt. He had walked through the town there at the head of the bay, smelling the salt air and recalling a season that might have been happier, though he now saw it as one of his many periods of adjustment to yet another changed time. He remembered the boat and a girl named Lynn and the seafood; these, and the fact that it was a small, unhurried place, permitting him to slip gradually into a new decade. Could something like this be what he really most needed now? he wondered. He shook his head. His grip tightened on the wheel as he negotiated a twisting descent.

Time to think. He needed to get to a safe place where he could work things out. Something was very wrong. He was missing important things. Cat had come too damned close. He ought to be able to shake him. This was still his world, for all of the changes. An alien beast should not be able to outwit him here. Time. He needed some time in which to work on it.

Vary the pattern, he had decided. If he had left some trace behind him in the boxes, some means by which his destination choices might become known, this move on his part should cancel that effect. He had rented the vehicle in Bantry and begun the northward drive along the trail he remembered. Passing through Glengarriff, he had continued onto this way toward Kenmare, moving through a countryside devoid of trip-boxes. For the moment, he felt free. There was only the night and the wind and the rocky prospect. He had been caught off balance by Cat's releasing him the previous evening. He had done nothing but improvise since then. What he had to come up with now was a plan, a general defense to sustain him through this trial. A plan . . .

A light in the distance. A pair of them now. Three . . . He raised a container and took a sip of coffee. His first mistake, he decided, had probably been in not tripping enough. He should have continued his movements to really cloud the trail. Cat had obviously been close enough to pick his destination from his mind. Even when he had jumped more than once, Cat could have been coming in as he was tripping out, and so could have learned the next stop.

Four . . . Kenmare would still be some distance beyond the first scattered farms and rural residences. This night was crisp. He descended a long slope. Abruptly, the trees were larger along the trailside.

The next time he would really mix it up. He would jump back and forth among so many places that the trail would be completely muddled. Yes, that was what he should have done at first—

The next time?

He screamed. The mental presence of Cat suddenly hung like the aroma of charred flesh about him.

"No—" he said, fighting to regain control of the vehicle which he had let swerve at his outburst.

He bounced across a field at a height of perhaps two feet, heading toward a steepening rise. Too abrupt a change in attitude would overturn the car.

Pulling the wheel around, he succeeded in veering away from the slope. Moments later, he was headed back toward the trail. Although he peered in every direction his light traveled, he saw no sign of the hunting beast.

Back on the trail once more, he accelerated. Shadows fled past. Tree limbs were stirred by the wind. Bits of fog drifting across his way were momentarily illuminated by the vehicle's beams. But this was all that he saw.

"Cat . . . ?" he finally said.

There was no reply. Was he so on edge that he had imagined that single phrase? The strain . . .

"Cat?"

It had seemed so real. He struggled to reconstruct his state of mind at the time of its occurrence. He supposed that he could have triggered it himself, but he did not like what this implied about his mental equipment.

He spun through a number of S-shaped curves, his eyes continuing their search on both sides of the trail.

So quickly . . . His confidence had been destroyed in an instant. Would he be seeing Cat behind every rock, every bush, from now on?

Why not?

"Cat!"

Yes.

Where are you? What are you doing?

Amusing myself. The point of this game must be maximum enjoyment, I have decided. It is good that you cooperate so well for this end.

How did you find me?

More easily than you might think. As I said, your cooperation is appreciated.

I do not understand.

Of course not. You tend to hide things from yourself.

What do you mean?

I know now that I can destroy you at any time, but I wish to prolong the pleasure. Keep running. I will strike at the most appropriate moment.

This makes no sense at all.

No. Because you will not let it. You are mine, hunter, whenever I choose.

Why?

He came onto a long, tree-lined curve. There seemed to be more lights far ahead.

I will tell you, and it will still not save you. You have changed from

114

what you once were. I see that within you which was not there in the old days. Do you know what you really want?

To beat you, Billy said. *And I will.*

No. Your greatest wish is to die.

That is not so!

You have given up on the thought of keeping up with your world. For a long while you have waited and wished for an appropriate way out of it. I have provided you with such an occasion. You think that you are running from me. Actually, you are rushing toward me. You make it easy for me, hunter.

Not true!

. . . And the lovely irony is that you do not admit it.

You have been in the minds of too many Californians. They're full of pop psychology . . .

. . . And your denial of it makes it that much easier for me.

You are trying to wear me down mentally. That's all.

No need for it.

You're bluffing. If you can strike now, let's see you do it.

Soon. Soon. Keep running.

He had to slow the vehicle for a series of turns. He continued to scan both sides of the trail. Cat must be near in order to reach him, but of course he had the advantage of straight-line travel whereas the trail—

Exactly.

Overhead, a piece of the night came loose, dropping from the top of a high boulder which leaned from the right. He tried to brake and cut to the left simultaneously.

A massive, jaguarlike form with a single, gleaming eye landed on the vehicle's hood forward and to the front. It was visible for but an instant, and then it sprang away.

The car tipped, its air cushion awry, and it was already turning onto its side before he left the trail. He fought with the wheel and the attitude control, already knowing that it was too late. There came a strong shock accompanied by a crunching noise, and he felt himself thrown forward.

D<small>EADLY, DEADLY, DEADLY</small> . . .
Kaleidoscope turning . . . Shifting pattern within unalterable
structure . . . Was it a mistake? There is pain with the power . . .
Time's friction at the edges . . . Center loosens, forms again
elsewhere . . . Unalterable? But— Turn outward. Here songs of self
erode the will till actions lie stillborn upon night's counterpane.
But— Again the movement . . . Will it hold beyond a catch of
moment? To fragment . . . Not kaleidoscope. No center. But
again . . . To form it will. To will it form. Structure . . . Pain . . .
Deadly, deadly . . . And lovely. Like a sleek, small dog . . . A plastic
statue . . . The notes of an organ, the first slug of gin on an empty
stomach . . . We settle again, farther than ever before . . . Center. The
light! . . . It is difficult being a god. The pain. The beauty. The terror
of selfless—Act! Yes. Center, center, center . . . Here? Deadly . . .

necess yet again from bridge of brainbow oyotecraven stare
decesis on landaway necessity timeslast the arnings ent and tided
turn yet beastfall nor mindstorms neither in their canceling sarved
cut the line that binds ecessity towarn and findaway twill open
pandorapack wishdearth amen amenuensis opend the mand of min
apend the pain of durthwursht vernichtung desiree tolight and eadly
dth cessity sesame

We are the key.

HE AWOKE TO STILLNESS AND THE
damp. The right side of his forehead was throbbing. His shoulders
ached and he became aware of the unnatural angle at which he lay.
His right arm felt wet. He opened his eyes and saw that the night still
lay upon the land. He stretched out his left hand and turned on the
interior light. As he did, shards of glass fell from his sleeve.

He saw then that the windshield was uncracked, and that the
wetness on his arm had been caused by the spilled remainder of his
coffee. He placed his fingertips on his forehead and felt no break in
the skin, but he could already detect a swelling in the sore area.

The vehicle lay on its right side, off the trail, its front end partly
crumpled against a tree. There were other trees and shrubs in the
vicinity, masking him somewhat from the trail. He looked upward
and to his left, and he could discover no reason for the broken side
window.

Then his gaze fell upon the headrest. There were four parallel
slash marks in the covering material beside his head, as from a set of
razor-sharp claws. He looked again at the broken side window.
Yes . . .

Cat?

Silence.

What are you waiting for?

He swung his feet about, set them carefully against the far door
and rose into the semblance of a standing position. Immediately he
grew dizzy and clutched at the steering wheel. When the spell
passed, he attempted to open the door. It yielded to his fourth effort
with a grinding, scraping sound. He caught hold of the frame and
drew himself upward, suddenly recalling having done something
similar with an old blue pickup truck, coming home from a Saturday
night in town an age ago.

There was a trail. Even in the dark he could read it. Cat had been there and gone. He felt the broken twigs, traced impressions in the earth with his fingertips. He followed it for perhaps twenty meters, heading off across the countryside. Then he rose and turned away.

What's your angle, Cat? What do you want now? he asked.

He heard only the wind. He walked slowly back to the roadway and continued along it. He was certain that only a few miles remained until he reached the town.

Perhaps ten minutes passed. No other traffic had come along, but he suspected that he was not alone. A large body seemed to be moving far off among the trees to his left, pacing him.

All right, Cat, he said. *There is no point to my taking evasive action now. If you are going to strike, strike. If not, enjoy the walk.*

There was no response, and he broke into a jog.

A feeling of nausea came over him before he had gone far. He ignored it and kept moving. He decided that it could be a reaction to the blow on his head.

But as he ran, his feelings came to include a fear that Cat was about to spring on him. He tried to thrust it away but it grew, and then he recognized its irrational roots.

I feel it, Cat. But I know what it is, he said. *What's the point of it? I'm still going on to Kenmare, unless you kill me. Are you just playing games?*

The intensity of the feelings increased. His breathing grew ragged. He felt a sudden urge to urinate. A sense of imminent doom was upon the trail for as far ahead as he could see.

Something like a small dog crossed his path. In that instant, his apprehensions vanished.

Was that the shadow I saw in the woods? he wondered. Is Cat long gone? Was my fear real, rather than induced?

Or is it all your doing, Cat? Is it your plan to make me doubt myself, to break me before you destroy me?

He jogged for a mile before a floatcar approached from the rear and drew abreast of him. Its driver offered him a ride into town.

118

As they moved forward, Billy felt within him the distant laughter of his pursuer.

• • •

To get out, to go away, to think. These were his preoccupations as he came into the town. He needed to escape for even a short while to someplace where Cat could not observe the workings of his mind. It was necessary that he continue his flight, try yet again to blur the trail sufficiently to gain respite for analysis of the situation, for planning.

He had the driver drop him at the trip-station. He assumed that somewhere Cat was reading his mind to learn his destination. He began chanting softly in Navajo, a section of the Blessingway. He entered the station and moved toward a booth. The place's only occupant was an old man seated on a wooden bench against the side wall to his right. The man looked up from his news printout and nodded to him.

" 'Evening," the man said.

He entered the booth and pressed the coordinates for Victoria Station.

. . . in beauty.

Now to Munich . . .

. . . all about me.

He cleaned himself in the washroom there and tripped to Rome.

. . . to the right of me.

He had a sandwich and a glass of wine.

. . . to the left of me.

He tripped to Ankara. For a time, he stood outside the terminal and watched the sun rising upon a hot, dusty day.

. . . before me.

He tripped to Al Hillah in Saudi Arabia, and from there to a bank of booths in the Rab al Khāli National Petroleum Forest.

Yes. Here, he decided, stepping forth among the great-leafed, towering trees, their barks scaled and brown and ringing in the wind. He followed a marked footpath through their shade.

119

Here, amid Freeman Dyson's old dream, he thought, he might be able to feel his way to something that he needed to know, here in what had once been known as the Empty Quarter, now an enormous forest of genetically tailored trees larger than redwoods, their sap rising, their programed metabolism synthesizing petroleum which flowed downward through a special set of vessels into roots which formed a living network of pipelines, connecting at various points to an artificial pipeline which conveyed it to the vast storage areas which constituted one of the world's great petroleum reserves, against those functions which still required the substance. They filled what had once been a wasteland, utilizing the abundant sunlight available there. Self-repairing and timeless against the blue of the sky, they were both natural and the product of the technology which informed the planet's culture, as surely as the trees of the street parks which delivered their own products, or the data net which, had he not disassociated himself from it, could at this moment deliver to him almost any information he needed.

Almost. Some things had to be worked out alone. But here, in this combination of the old and the new, the primitive and the modern, he felt more at ease than he had since the entire business began. There were even birds singing in the branches. . . .

He walked for a long while through the forest, pausing when he came to a small cleared area containing a pair of picnic tables, a waste bin, a shed. He looked into the shed: foresters' maintenance equipment—power diggers, pickaxes, saws; chains and cables; gloves and climbing spikes. It was dusty, and spiderwebs like gossamer bridges connected each to each.

He closed the door and moved away, sniffed the air and looked around. He seated himself with his back to the bole of a middle-sized tree, some few stalks of coarse saffron and lime grass tufted about the hillock among the roots. He filled his pipe and lit it.

Cat wanted his death and had tried to convince him that he did, too. The idea seemed absurd, but he looked at it more closely. Much of the universe was one's adversary. He had learned that as a boy.

One took precautions and hoped for the best. Time was flowing water, neither good nor evil and not to be grasped. One could cup one's hand and hold a little of it for a while, and that was all. It had become a torrent, though, in the past decade of his own life—which covered about thirty years of real time—and he could contain none of it. The big world had changed rapidly during that span. The dancers had exchanged masks; he could no longer identify the enemies.

Save for Cat.

But that was unfair, he saw, even to Cat. Cat he could understand. Cat was simple, monomaniacal, in his desire. The rest of the world was dangerous in changing and complicated ways, though it generally lacked malice and premeditation. It was an adversary, not an enemy. Cat was the enemy. The universe was that which ground down and rolled over one. And now . . .

The tempo had increased. He had felt it all his life, from his first school days on, intensifying, like a drumbeat. There had been lapses, true; periods when he had come to terms with the new rhythms. But now— He felt tired. The last responses were no longer appropriate, not even among his own people. Looking back, he saw that he had felt best on those occasions when he had gone away, into the timeless places among the stars, hunting. It was the return that was always the shock. Now . . . now he just wanted to rest. Or to go away again, even though the next return . . .

Dora. It had been peaceful with Dora also. But that did not help him now. Thinking of Dora now only caused him to look away from the real problems. Did he really want to die? Was Cat right?

He could almost hear singing within the unnatural tree which paralleled his backbone, vibrations humming along his nerves.

To want to run away, to want to rest and change no more . . . Perhaps . . .

He bit down hard on the pipestem. He did not like all of this *bellicano* thinking, this hunting for hidden motives. But . . .

Perhaps there was something to it. His jaw muscles relaxed again.

121

If the hidden sources of his feelings did equal what Cat had been talking about, he had been running toward death ever since Dora's fall and—

Dora? How did she figure into this part? No, let the dead rest and not trouble the living. It would be enough to admit that all of the changes in society itself—a society into which he had not been born but of which he had tried to make himself a part—were sufficiently overwhelming to have brought him to this point. Take it from there. What next? What did he really want? And what should he do about it?

Suddenly a memory unfolded, startling him with a knowledge he had possessed all along. After the shock of the recognition he grew depressed, for he knew then that Cat's words had been true.

Each time that he had fled by means of a trip-box he had had his ultimate destination at the back of his mind. All of the jumping about he had done before heading for his goal had been as nothing. Cat had needed but to read that final destination, to go there and begin patrolling the city, hunting first his mind and then his body. This seemed more than carelessness on his part. It was as if he had intentionally given himself to Cat and kept the information hidden from his own scrutiny. How could he trust himself to do anything now?

On the other hand, doing nothing could prove equally fatal. He was surprised at his sudden willingness to admit to a hidden death wish. He was determined not to yield to it, however, not in this duel with Cat. He puffed on his pipe and listened to the birds.

Had he this destination in mind when he had departed Kenmare on the first of this latest series of jumps? It seemed that he had. . . .

All right. He rose. He had to assume that Cat was aware of it and could put in an appearance at any time. The longer he remained here, the greater the beast's chances of finding him unprepared. He dusted off his trousers and muttered "Damn!" He still needed time to plan.

He slapped the side of the tree and headed across the picnic area

122

toward the trail. A huge crow darted past him and he halted. Thoughts of Black-god tumbled through his mind, and of the ways of the hunt.

The only trip-station in the area was the one he had used. Cat could emerge there at any moment, perhaps just as he was approaching. No, that would not do. Because he was defenseless, it was prudent to continue the flight. But the risk involved in attempting it right now seemed too high.

IT CAME DOWN FROM UTAH AND Colorado, and it was big and black and nasty. When it attacked, the people fled for cover and waited. It lashed and splashed and filled gullies. From Lake Powell through the Carrizos it boiled and roared. It licked Shiprock with tongues of flame. The patches of white in the high places were diminished beneath its slavering. It rolled across the land and hauled itself over the mountain peaks. Its breath was fast and sharp, snapping limbs from pine trees, twisting piñons. Arroyos became muddy snakes. There were mists, and in some places rainbows. The thunder no longer slept. Legends could no longer be told.

> *The Keeper of Clouds has unpenned his charges.*
> *The Keeper of Winds has unlocked his gates.*
> *The Keeper of Waters has opened the sky.*
> *The Keeper of Lightnings waves his lances.*
> *The Keeper of Satellites has observed,*
> *"One hundred percent of probability of precipitation."*

HE EMERGED FROM THE TRIP-BOX AND
looked about. He stood for a time as if listening. Then he dropped to
all fours and entered the forest, his form altering as he advanced. He
had detected the mind which he sought. It was filled again with the
feelings of that chanting and all of the obscure imagery associated
with it. But while this masked the underlying thoughts it in no way
obscured the direction and location of the thinker. Finding the body
should not be all that difficult.

His movements grew more and more graceful as the lines of his
body flowed to assume the catlike form he favored. His eye sparkled
like a liquid thing. His incisors overhung his lower lip by several
inches. They, too, sparkled. His passage among the great petroleum
trees was almost soundless. Whenever he froze and sought
impressions he became almost invisible within the dappled patterns
of light and shadow.

On one such occasion a leaf fell. Cat pounced upon it, a living
blur. He straightened then and shook his head. He stared at the leaf.
Then he started forward again.

Perhaps this should be the time. The game was not proving as
complex as he had hoped. If there were no interesting fight or flight,
if nothing exciting happened this time, it might be best to conclude
things here. The hunter seemed to have lost his edge, seemed weary,
too troubled to provide the necessary struggle.

He glared for a moment at the black bird which cried out above
his head, circling and then darting away.

Come back, dearie. Just for a moment. Come look again.

But the bird was gone.

Cat flicked his wide tail and pressed on across a low spongy
section of forest floor. It was not that much farther. . . . He increased
his pace and did not slow again until he was near to the picnic area.
Then he studied and circled and studied again.

The man was just sitting there, his back against a picnic bench, smoking his pipe, his mind filled with that senseless chant. It was almost too easy, but this was the way he had read him earlier: willfully careless, ready to die. Still . . .

There was no sport in it. A few taunts, and perhaps he will bolt.

You see. It is as I said. When you run from me you approach me. Why was I not freed at some other time, when you still cared to live?

The hunter did not reply. The chant continued.

So you have admitted the truth. You accept what I told you. Is that your death song that you sing?

Again there was no response.

Very well. I see no reason to prolong things, hunter.

Cat passed among the trees and entered the cleared area.

Last chance. Will you not at least draw your knife?

Billy stood and turned slowly to face him.

At last. You are awake. Are you going to run?

Billy did not move. Cat bounded forward. There followed a splintering sound.

When the ground gave way beneath the beast, the moment was frozen in Billy's mind. He had had some doubt as to the appropriate width when wielding the power shovel to dig the trench which encircled him. As its covering gave way and Cat vanished below he was pleased that his estimate had proven adequate. He moved immediately to bridge it with the picnic table.

You will not hold me here for long, hunter, Cat told him from below.

Long enough, I hope.

Billy crossed over the trench and emptied the wastebin against the trunk of a nearby tree. He struck a light and set it to the heap of papers.

What are you doing?

If one of these trees goes up, the whole area burns, he said. *They're all connected below and full of inflammables. You won't make it back to the box if you let this burn.*

Billy turned and began running.

125

Congratulations, Cat told him. *You have made it interesting again.*
Good-bye, Billy said.
Not quite. We've an appointment.

He ran on until the trip-box was in sight. Rushing into it, he inserted his strip, activating the control and punched coordinates at random without looking at them.

You have bought respite, Cat told him. *But at another level you have betrayed yourself again.*

Have I? Billy answered, as the forest blurred.

He walks in a twilight land amid jungle-shrouded cities. The cries of unseen birds come to him across the shimmering air. It is pleasantly warm, and there is a smell of dampness and decay. His path is a glistening ribbon among ruins which appear less and less ruined as he advances. He smells burning copal and his guide gives him a strange beverage to drink. Colors flash beneath his feet and his way becomes bright red. They come at length to a pyramid atop which a blue man is held stretched across a stone by four others. Billy watches as a man in a high headdress cuts open the blue man's chest and removes the heart. He sips his drink and continues to watch as the heart is passed to another man who uses it to anoint the faces of statues. The body is then cast down the steps to where a crowd of people waits. There, another man very carefully removes the skin, its blue now streaked with red, dons it like a robe and commences dancing. The other people now fall upon the remains and begin eating, save for the hands and the feet, which are removed and set aside. His guide departs for a moment to join the crowd, returning moments later, bringing him something and indicating that he should eat. He chews

126

mechanically, washing it down with the balché. *He looks up, realizing suddenly that Dora is his guide. "On the fifth day of* Uayeb *my true love gave to me . . ." She is not smiling. Her face is, in fact, without expression as she turns away, beckoning for him to follow. The blood-red way leads at length to a gaping cave-mouth. They halt before it, and he can see that within there are statues at either hand—fanged, scrolls upon their foreheads, dark circles about their eyes. As he stares, he becomes aware of people moving about slowly inside. They are placing bowls of copal, tobacco and maize upon a low altar. They are chanting softly in words which he does not understand. She leads him across the threshold, and he sees now that the place is illuminated by candlelight. He smells incense as he stands listening to the prayers. He is given to drink a beverage of corn gruel and honey at each pausing between rituals. He sits with his back against the rock, listening, tracing circles upon the floor with his fingertip. He is given another gourd of* balché *to drink. As he raises it to his lips he looks upward and pauses. It is not Dora who has brought him the drink but a powerful youth, clad in the old manner of the Dineh. At this person's back there stands another man—larger and even stronger-looking. He is similarly garbed, and the resemblance between the two is striking. "You seem familiar," Billy tells them. The first man smiles. "We are the slayers of the giants Seven-Macaws, Zipacna and Cabracan," he answers. "It was we," says the other, "who journeyed down the steps to Xibalba, crossing the River of Corruption and the River of Blood. We followed the Black Path to the House of the Lords of Death." The other nods. "We played strange games with them, both winning and losing," he says. And they say in unison, "We slew the Lords Hun-Came and Vucub-Came and ascended into light." Billy sips his* balché. *"You remind me," he says to the younger one, "of Tobadzichini, and you," to the other, "of Nayenezgani, the Warrior Twins of my people, as I always thought they must look." The two smile. "This is true," they say, "for we get around a lot. Down here we are known as Hunahpu and Xbalanque. Rise now to your feet and look off yonder into the darker places." He gets up and looks to the rear of the grotto. He sees*

127

there a trail leading downward. Dora stands upon it, staring at him. "Follow," says Hunahpu. "Follow," says Xbalanque. She begins to move away. As he turns and follows after her, he hears the cry of a bird. . . .

$\mathbf{B}$ILLY STEPPED FROM THE TRIP-BOX and looked about. It was dark, with a tropical brilliance to the stars. The air was cool and damp, bearing smells he had long associated with jungle foliage. The coolness seemed to indicate that the night was nearing its end.

He passed beyond the station's partitioning, where he read the sign which identified it. Yes. Things were as he had sensed them. He had come to the great archaeological park of Chichén Itzá.

He stood upon a low hill. Narrow trails led off in many directions. These paths were faintly illuminated, and here and there he saw people passing slowly along them. He could discern the massive dark forms of the ancient structures themselves, more solid and deep than the night's lesser gloom. Periodically, some portion of ruin would be brilliantly lighted for several minutes, for the benefit of night-viewers. He recalled reading somewhere that this ran through a regular cycle, its schedule available at various points along the way, along with computerized commentary and the answering of questions concerning the place.

He began walking. The ruin was big and dark and quiet and Indian. It comforted him to pass along its ways. Cat could not find him here. This he knew. He also understood Cat's parting words. He had betrayed himself, in a sense, for his final destination had been present in his mind even as he had struck the random coordinates which had brought him here. When he finally journeyed to that last place it would be to face his enemy.

He laughed softly then. There was nothing to prevent his remaining here until Cat's time limit had run out.

Some of the more fragile ruins he passed were protected by force fields, others permitted entry, climbing, wandering. He was reminded of this as he brushed against a force screen—soft, harder, harder, impenetrable. It reminded him of Cat's cage back at the Institute. Cat's had also been electrified, however, providing shocks which increased in direct proportion to the intensity of the pressure from within. Cat had seldom brushed against it, though, because of his peculiar sensitivity to electrical currents. In fact, that was how Billy had captured him—accidentally, when Cat had collided with the electrified force screen which had surrounded one of the base camps during an attempt at backtracking and ambush. The memory suddenly gave rise to a new train of thought.

A light flashed on far to his right, and he halted and stared. He had never been here before, but he had seen pictures, had read about the place. It was the Temple of the Warriors that he beheld, a bristling of columns before it, their shadows black slashes upon its forward wall. He began to move toward it.

The light went out before he got there, but he had the location as well as the image fixed in his mind. He continued until he was very near, and when he discovered that no force field blocked his way he passed among the styli and began to climb the steep stair on its forward face.

When he reached the level area at the top he located himself to what he took to be the east and sat down, his back against the wall of the smaller structure situated at the center. He thought of Cat and of the death wish that was defeating him because he could not adapt, because he was no longer Navajo. Or was that true? He thought of his recent years of withdrawal. Now they seemed filled with ashes. But his people had many times tasted the ashes of fear and suffering, sorrow and submission, yet they had never lost their dignity nor all

129

of their pride. Sometimes cynical, often defiant, they had survived. Something of this must still be with him, to match against his own death prayer. He dozed then and had a peculiar dream which he could not later recall in its entirety.

When he woke the sun was rising. He watched the waves of color precede it into the world. It was true that there was nothing to prevent his remaining here until Cat's time limit had run out. He knew that he would not do this. He would go on to face his *chindi*.

. . . After breakfast, he decided. After breakfast.

"I DON'T CARE!" MERCY SPENDER said, raising the bottle with one hand, the glass with the other. "I've got to have another drink!"

Elizabeth Brooke laid a hand upon her shoulder.

"I really don't think you should, dear. Not just now, anyhow. You're agitated and—"

"I know! That's why I want it!"

With a snapping sound, the bottom fell out of the bottle. The gin raced shards of glass to the floor. The odor of juniper berries drifted upward.

"What . . . ?"

Walter Sands smiled.

"Mean of me," he said. "But we still need you. I know you'd like to go and rest in the home again. It will be harder for us if you drop out now, though. Wait a while."

Mercy stared downward. A look of anger passed and her eyes brimmed, sparkled.

"It's silly," she said then. "If he wants to die, let him."

"It's not that simple. He's not that simple," Ironbear said. "And we owe him."

"*I* don't owe him anything," she said, "and we don't even know what to do, really. I—" Then, "We all have something that hurts, I guess," she said. "Maybe . . . Okay. I'll take some tea."

"I wonder what hurts the thing that's after him?" Fisher asked.

"The data are incomplete on the ecology of the place it comes from," Mancin said.

"Then there is only one way to find out, isn't there?" asked Ironbear. "Go to the source."

"Ridiculous," Fisher said. "It's hard enough touching a human who's gone primitive. The beast seems able to do it at short ranges because they share some bond. But to go after the thing itself and then—I couldn't."

"Neither could I," said Elizabeth. "None of us could. But *we* might be able to."

"We? Us? Together? Again? It could be dangerous. After that last time—"

"Again."

"We don't even know where the cat-thing is."

"Walford's man can order another check on TripCo's computer network. Locate Singer again and the beast will soon be there."

"And what good would that do us?"

"We won't know till we get that information and give it a try."

"I don't like this," said Fisher. "We could get hurt. It's a damned alien place you're talking about. I touched one of the Strageans yesterday and had a headache for half an hour afterwards. Couldn't even see straight. And they're similar to us in a lot of ways.

"We can always back out if it gets too rough."

"I've got a bad feeling about this," Mercy said, "but I guess it does seem like the Christian thing to do."

"The hell with that. Is it going to do any good?"

"Maybe you're right," Mancin said. "It doesn't seem all that promising when you analyze it. Let's tell Walford how Singer did it, tell him about the beast and the deal they made. Then get the computer check to narrow the field. They can send an armed force after it."

"Send it after the thing that killed the thing an armed force couldn't stop?"

"Let's locate them," Ironbear said, "find out what we can and then decide."

"That much makes sense," Sands said. "I'll go along with it."

"So will I," said Elizabeth.

Mancin glanced at Fisher.

"Looks as if we're outvoted," he said, sighing. "Okay."

Fisher nodded.

"Call Tedders. Run it through TripCo. I'll be with you."

BILLY STEPPED THROUGH INTO HIS hogan, leaving the transport slip in place. He switched on the guard and turned off the buzzer. He was not receiving calls just now.

His secretary unit told him that Edwin Tedders had called several times. Would he please call back? Another caller left no name, only the message, "They grew them with insulation, I learned. You knew that, didn't you?"

He turned on the coffee maker, undressed and stepped into the shower. As he was vibrated clean, he heard the rumble of thunder above the cries of the nozzles.

When he had emerged and dressed himself in warmer clothing he took his coffee out onto his porch. The sky was gray to the north and curtains of rain hung there. A fast wind fled past him. To the south and the east the sky was clear. Light clouds drifted in the west. He watched the rolling weeds and listened to the wind for a time, finished his coffee and returned to the inside.

Billy picked up the weapon and checked it over. Old-fashioned. A tazer, it was called, firing a pronged cable and delivering a strong electrical jolt at the far end. They had fancier things now which ionized a path through the air and sent their charge along it. But this would do. He had used a similar device on Cat before, once he had learned his weakness.

Then he honed a foot-long Bowie knife and threaded his belt through the slits in its sheath. He inspected an old 30.06 he had kept in perfect condition. If he could succeed in stunning Cat, it could pump sufficient rounds through that tough hide to hit vital organs, he knew. On the other hand, the weapon was fairly heavy. He finally selected a half-meter laser snub-gun, less accurate but equally lethal. He planned on using it at close range, anyway. That decided, he set to putting together a light pack with minimal gear for the trek he had in mind. When everything was assembled, he set an alarm, stretched out on his bedroll and slept for two hours.

When the buzzer roused him the rain was drumming on the roof. He donned a waterproof fleece-lined jacket, shouldered his pack, slung his weapons and found a hat. Then he crossed to his communications unit, checked a number and punched it.

Shortly the screen came to life, and Susan Yellowcloud's wide face appeared before him.

"Azaethlin!" she said. She brushed back a strand of hair and smiled. "It's been a couple of years."

"Yes," he said, and he exchanged greetings and a bit of small talk. "Raining over your way?" he finally asked.

"Looks as if it's about to."

"I need to get over to the north rim," he told her. "You're the closest person I know to the spot I have in mind. Okay if I come over?"

"Sure. Get in your box and I'll key ours."

He stepped in, pocketed his strip and punched TRANS.

133

He came through in the corner of a cluttered living room. Jimmy Yellowcloud arose from a chair set before a viewscreen to press palms with him. He was short, wide-shouldered, thick around the waist.

"Hosteen Singer," he said. "Have a cup of coffee with us."

"All right," Billy said.

As they drank it, Jimmy remarked, "You said you're going over to the canyon?"

"Yes."

"Not down in it, I hope."

"I'm going down in it."

"The spring flooding's started."

"I'd guessed."

"Nasty-looking gun. Could I see it?"

"Here."

"Hey, laser! You could punch another hole in Window Rock with this thing. It's old, isn't it?"

"About eighty years. I don't think they make them just like that anymore."

He passed it back.

"Hunting something?"

"Sort of."

They sat in silence for a time, then, "I'll drive you over to wherever you want on the rim," he said.

"Thanks."

Jimmy took another sip of coffee.

"Going to be down there long?" he asked.

"Hard to say."

"We don't see much of you these days."

"Been keeping to myself."

Jimmy laughed.

"You ought to marry my wife's sister and come live over here."

"She pretty?" Billy asked.

"You bet. Good cook, too."

"Do I know her?"

134

"I don't think so. We'll have to have a squaw dance."

A sudden drumming of rain occurred on the north side of the house.

"Here it comes," Jimmy said. "Don't suppose you'd care to wait till it stops?"

Billy chuckled.

"Could be days. You'd go broke feeding me."

"We could play cards. Not much else for a ranger to do this time of year."

Billy finished his coffee.

"You could learn to make jewelry—conchos, bracelets, rings."

"My hands just don't go for that."

Jimmy put down his cup.

"Nothing else to do. I might as well change clothes and go along with you. I've got a high-powered hunting rifle with a radar sight. Knock over an elephant."

Billy traced a design on the tabletop.

"Not this time," he said.

"All right. Guess we'd better get going then."

"Guess we should."

• • •

He let Jimmy drop him on the northward bulge of the rim above the area containing the Antelope House ruin. Since he had had the ride he had decided to come this much farther eastward. Had he walked over, he would have descended at a point several miles farther to the west. Jimmy would have taken him even farther eastward had he wished, but that would have been less useful, starting him at a place beyond the point where Black Rock Canyon branched off from Canyon del Muerto proper. He wanted to pass that point on foot and confuse the trail there. If he made things too easy Cat would become suspicious.

Staring downward into the broad, serpentine canyon, he saw a wide band of dully gleaming water passing down its center, as he had suspected. It was not yet as deep as he had seen it on occasions in the past, rushing with the seasonal meltoff between orange,

135

salmon and gray walls, splashing the bases of obelisklike stands of stone, cascading over irregularities, rippling about boulders, bearing the mud and detritus of its passage on toward the Chinle Wash, creating pockets of quicksand all over the canyon floor. Several hundred of the People made their homes there during the warmer months, but they all moved out for the winter. The place would be deserted now.

A light rain was falling, making the wall rocks slippery. He cast about for the safest way down. There, to the left.

He moved to the spot he had selected and studied it more closely. Yes. It could be done. He checked his pack and commenced the descent. The way led down to the high, firm talus slope which followed the wall's base.

Partway down, he paused to adjust his pack, brush off moisture and look sideways and back in at the petroglyph of a life-sized antelope. There were a number of them about, along with those of other quadrupeds, turkeys, human figures, concentric circles; some of them continued onto the fourth-story level of the large ruin built against the base of the cliff. His people had done none of these. They went back to the Great Pueblo period, in the twelfth to fourteenth centuries, work of the old Anasazi. He worked his way down and around, and the going suddenly became easier. Here the slant and overhang of the wall protected him from the rainfall.

When he reached the bottom he turned to the east, the splashing waters off to the right, faded grasses and scrubby trees about him on the slope. He made no effort to conceal his passage but advanced with long, purposeful strides. Across the water at the base of the opposite cliff stood Battle Cove Ruin, a small masonry structure with white, red, yellow and green petroglyphs. It, too, went back to the Great Pueblo days. As a boy he might have feared such places, feared rousing the vengeful spirits of the Old Ones. On the other hand, he would probably have gone through them on a dare, he decided.

Jagged lightning danced somewhere in the east—*ikne'eka'a*. A slow roll of thunder followed. He felt that Cat was probably in

Arizona by now, having seen the Canyon de Chelly Monument in his mind, the Canyon del Muerto branch in particular. Locating the trip-box at the Thunderbird Lodge would be kind of esoteric, though. Doubtless Cat would have arrived by way of Chinle—which meant that he still had a long way to come, even if he had gotten in a few hours ago.

Good. Black Rock Canyon was not that far ahead.

. . .

The track of the wind upon my fingertips,
mark of my mortality.
The track of the rain upon my hand,
mark of the waiting world.
A song that rises unbidden within me,
mark of my spirit.
The light of that half-place
where his mount danced for Crazy Horse,
mark of that other world
where powers still walk, stones talk
and nothing is what it seems to be.
We will meet in an old place.
The earth will tremble. The stones will drink.
Things forgotten are shadows.
The shadows will be as real
as wind and rain and song and light,
there in the old place.
Spider Woman atop your rock,
I would greet you,
but I am going the other way.
Only a fool would pursue a Navajo
into the Canyon of Death.
Only a fool would go there at all
when the waters are running.
I am going to an old place.
He who follows must go there, too.
Windmark, raintouch, songrise, light,

137

with me, on me, in me, about me.
It is good to be a fool when the time is right.
I am a son of the Sun
and Changing Woman.
I go to an old place.
Na-ya!

. . .

When Cat emerged from the trip-box at Chinle he wore a dark
cloak, glasses and floppy-hat disguise. The station was empty now,
though he could see a couple of minutes into the past in a limited
fashion with his infrared vision and knew from the heat signatures
that two people had recently been standing inside the doorway for a
while. He moved forward and looked outside. Yes. A man and a
woman were walking away. Presumably one had met the other here
and they had stood talking for a time before going on their way. As
he watched, they crossed the street and entered a café to his left.
Their thoughts served to remind him that for many hours he had
been growing hungry. Without moving, his eye also took in countless
images of the nearby wall map. He was getting the idea of such
things better now, and he would remember all of the markings on
this one. When he saw something which corresponded to a feature,
he would have his directions, though he felt he already knew them.
In the meantime, he would follow his feelings and his hunger while
gaining impressions.

He departed the station. Half of the sky was overcast and the
clouds seemed to be moving to cover more. He felt the dampness
and negative ionization in the air.

He passed along the street. Three men rounded the corner and
stared at him for an unusually long while. *Stranger. Odd. Very odd,*
he read. *Something funny about that one, the way he moves . . .*
Images then. Childhood fears. Old stories. Similar in ways to Billy's
stream of consciousness.

More people approaching from the rear. No design to their
movement in his direction. But the same curiosity flowing.

He selected. He broadcast fears and old forebodings: *Flee! Man-*

wolf, shapeshifter! Gnawer of corpses! I will shoot corruption into your bodies, blow the dust of corpses into your lungs. Wolf, wearer of the skin. I will track you and rend you!

The men at his back hastily turned into an open shop. Those before him halted, then quickly crossed the street. Almost amused, he continued to broadcast the feelings for a time after they had departed. It cleared the way before him. People would begin to emerge from buildings and halt, then return within, as if suddenly recalling something undone inside, experiencing the resurgence of childhood fears. Better to give in and rationalize later than to brave them out for no reason.

But they are real, he reflected. I *am* the shapeshifter who could strike you down without effort. I could have stepped from your nightmare legends. . . .

He picked the direction of the Chinle Wash from a retreating mind, turned at the next corner and again at the following one.

Silly. No one in sight now. There will be no trouble, he decided.

Stretching and contracting, he bent forward. Soon he was loping along the street. Not far, not too far. This way was indeed north. The town thinned out, fell away. He departed the roadway, ran beside it, cut across country. Better, better. Soon now. Yes. Downhill. Trees and desiccated grasses. A faint flash of light. Much later, a soft growl from the eastern sky.

Down, down into a barrenness of sand and moist earth, detached tree limbs and half-sunken stones. Firm enough, firm enough to run and—

He halted. Ahead, a primitive sentience, wandering. Automatically he fell into a stalking mode of progress. Hunger remembered in this almost delicious spot, save for the moisture. Slow now, beyond the next bend . . .

He halted again as soon as he saw the canine, a lean, black dog, sniffing about the heaps of rubble. Parts of it might do, if he diluted them. . . .

He sprang forward. The dog did not even raise its head until his third bounding movement, and by then it was too late. It let out one short whimpering noise before the projected feelings hit it, and then Cat's left paw shattered its spine.

Cat raised his muzzle from tearing at the carcass and swiveled his head so as to cover every direction, including straight up, with his many-faceted gaze. Nothing. Nothing moving but the wind and its consequences. Yet . . . He had felt as if something were watching him. But no.

He fell to tearing the bones free, breaking them, grinding them, swallowing them along with large gulps of sand. Not as good as crunching the tube-crawlers back home, but better than the synthetic fare they had given him at the Institute. Much better. In his mind, he roamed again the dry plains, fearing nothing but—

What? Again. He shook himself and ran his gaze entirely around the horizon. There was nothing, yet he felt as if something were stalking him.

He dropped into a lower position, spitting out pieces of dog, baring his fangs, listening, watching. What could there be to fear? There was nothing on this planet that he would not face. Yet he felt menaced by something he did not understand. Even when he had met with *krel,* long ago, he had known where he stood. Now, though . . .

He sent forth a paralyzing wave of feelings and waited. Nothing. No indication that anything had felt it. Could this be like dreaming?

Time ticked nets about him. The sky flared briefly beyond his right shoulder.

Gradually the tension went out of him. Gone now. Strange. Very strange. Could it be something about this place?

He finished his meal, thinking again of the days of the hunt on the plains of his own world, where only one thing could cause such uneasiness in him. . . .

It struck.

Whatever it was, it fell upon him like a boulder out of nowhere. He bunched his legs beneath him and sprang straight up into the air when it hit, head thrown back, a sharp hissing noise passing his throat. For an instant, his vision swam and the world grew dim. But already his mind was spinning. This he could understand, after a fashion.

Among his kind the mating battles were always preceded by a psychic assault from the challenger. This was somehow similar, and he possessed the equipment to join it.

He could not tell exactly what it was doing inside his head, but he struck at it with all of his hate, with the desire to rend. And then it was gone.

He fell across the carcass of the dog, teeth still bared, slipping back into an earlier mode of existence. Where was the other? When would he strike? He ranged with all of his senses about the area, waiting. But there was nothing there.

After a long while, the tension flowed away. Nothing was coming. Whatever it had been, it was not one of his own kind, and it had not been a battle challenge that he had felt. It troubled him that there was something in the area which he did not understand. He turned toward the north and began walking.

• • •

Mercy Spender and Charles Fisher, who sat at either side of him, reached to catch hold of Walter Sands's shoulders as he slumped forward.

"Get him up onto the table—quick!" Elizabeth said.

"He just fainted," Fisher said. "I think we ought to lower his head."

"Listen to his chest! I was still with him. I felt his heart stop."

"Oh, my! Somebody give us a hand!"

They moved him onto the table and listened for a heartbeat, but there was none. Mercy began hammering on his chest.

"You know what you're doing?" Ironbear asked her.

"Yes. I started nursing training once," she grunted. "I remember this part. Somebody send for help."

Elizabeth crossed to the intercom.

"I didn't know he had a bad heart," Fisher said.

"I don't think he did either," Mancin replied, "or we'd probably have learned that when we gave each other a look. The shock when the thing struck back must have gotten to him. We shouldn't have let Ironbear talk us into going in."

"Not his fault," Mercy said, still working.

"And we all agreed," Fisher said. "The time seemed perfect, while it was remembering. And we did learn something . . ."

Elizabeth reached Tedders. They grew silent as they listened to her relay the information.

"Just a moment ago. Just a moment ago," Fisher said, "and he was with us."

"It seems as if he still is," Mancin said.

"We're going to have to try to reach Singer," Elizabeth said, crossing the room and taking her seat again.

"That's going to be hard—and what do we really have to tell him?" Fisher asked.

"Everything we know," Ironbear said.

"And who knows what form it would take, that strange state of mind he's in?" Mercy asked. "We might be better off simply calling for that force Mancin suggested."

"Maybe we should do both," Elizabeth said. "But if we don't try helping him ourselves, then Walter's attack was for nothing."

"I'll be with you," Mercy said, "when we do. Somebody's going to have to take over here pretty soon, though, till the medics trip through. I'm getting tired."

"I'll try," Fisher said. "Let me watch how you do it."

"I'd better learn, too," Mancin said, moving nearer. "I do still seem to feel his presence, weakly. Maybe that's a good sign."

Sounds of hammering continued downstairs, from where a shattered wall was being replaced.

．．．

He crossed the water above a small cascade, knowing things would be relatively solid at its top. Then he moved along the southern talus slope, leaving a clear trail. He entered Black Rock Canyon and continued into it for perhaps half a mile. The rain came down steadily upon him and the wind made a singing sound high overhead. He saw a cluster of rocks come loose from the northern

142

wall far ahead, sliding and bumping to the floor of the canyon, splashing into the stream.

Keeping watch on driftwood heaps, he located a stick sufficient for his purpose. He walked near the water's edge for a time, then headed up onto a long rocky shelf where his footprints soon vanished. He immediately began to backtrack, walking in his own prints until he stood beside the water again. He entered it then, probing with the stick for quicksand pockets, and made his way back to the canyon's mouth.

Emerging, he crossed the main stream to its north bank, turned to his right and continued on along Canyon del Muerto toward Standing Cow Ruin, concealing his trail as he went, for the next half-mile. He found that he liked the feeling of being alone again in this gigantic gorge. The stream was wider here, deeper. His mind went back to the story he had heard as a boy, of the time of the fear of the flooding of the world. Who was that old singer? Up around Kayenta, back in the 1920s . . . The old man had been struck by lightning and left for dead. But he had recovered several days later, bearing a purported message from the gods, a message that the world was about to be flooded. In that normal laws and taboos no longer apply to a person who has lived through a lightning-stroke, he was paid special heed. People believed him and fled with their flocks to Black Mountain. But the water did not come, and the cornfields of those who fled dried and died under the summer sun. A shaman with a vision that did not pay off.

Billy chuckled. What was it the Yellowclouds had called him? "Azaethlin"–"medicine man." We aren't always that reliable, he thought, given to the same passions and misapprehensions as others. Medicine man, heal thyself.

He started past a "wish pile" of rocks and juniper twigs, halted, went back and added a stone to it. Why not? It was there.

In time, he came to Standing Cow Ruin, one of the largest ruins in the canyons. It stood against the north wall beneath a huge overhang. The remains of its walls covered an area more than four hundred feet long, built partly around immense boulders. It, too, went back to the Great Pueblo days, containing three kivas and many rooms. But there were also Navajo log-and-earth storage bins and Navajo paintings along with those of the Anasazi. He went nearer, to view again the white, yellow and black renderings of people with arms upraised, the humpbacked archer, circles, circles and more circles, the animals. . . . And there, high up above a ledge to his left, was one of purely Navajo creation, and most interesting to him. Mounted, cloaked, wearing flat-brimmed hats, carrying rifles, was a procession of Spaniards, two of them firing at an Indian. It was believed to represent the soldiers of Lieutenant Anthony Narbona who fought the Navajos at Massacre Cave in 1805. And below that, at the base of the cliff, were other horsemen and a mounted U.S. cavalryman of the 1860s. As he watched, they seemed to move.

He rubbed his eyes. They really were moving. And it seemed as if he had just heard gunshots. The figures were three-dimensional, solid now, riding across a sandy waste. . . .

"Always down on us, aren't you?" he said to them and to the world at large.

He heard curses in Spanish. When he lowered his eyes to the other figure, he heard a trumpet sounding a cavalry charge. The great rock walls seemed to melt away about him and the waters grew silent. He was staring now at a totally different landscape—bleak, barren and terribly bright. He raised his eyes to a sun which blazed almost whitely from overhead. A part of him stood aside, wondering how this thing could be. But the rest of him was engaged in the vision.

He seemed to hear the sound of a drum as he watched them ride across that alien desert. It was increasing steadily in tempo. Then, when it had reached an almost frantic throbbing, the sands erupted before the leading horseman and a large, translucent, triangular shape reared suddenly before him, leaning forward to enfold both horse and rider with slick membranous wings. More of them exploded into view along the column, shrugging sands which yellowed the air, falling upon the other riders and their mounts, enveloping them, dragging them downward to settle as quivering,

144

gleaming, rocklike lumps on the barren landscape. Even the cavalryman, now brandishing his saber, met a similar fate, to the notes of the trumpet and the drum.

Of course.

What other fate might be expected when one encountered a *krel,* let alone a whole crowd of them? He had given up quickly on any notion of bringing one back to the Institute. Two close calls, and he had decided that they were too damned dangerous. That world of Cat's had bred some very vicious creatures. . . .

Cat. Speak of the Devil . . . There was Cat crossing the plain, lithe power personified. . . .

Again, amid a shower of sand, the *krel* rose. Cat drew back, rearing, forelimbs lengthening, slashing. They came together and Cat struggled to draw away. . . .

With the sound of a single drumbeat, the scene faded. He was staring at anthropomorphic figures, horses and the large Standing Cow. He heard the sounds of the water at his back.

Peculiar, but he had known stranger things over the years, and he had always felt that a kind of power dwelled in the old places. Something about this manifestation of it seemed heartening, and so he took it as a good omen. He chanted a brief song of thanks for the vision and turned to continue along his way. The shadows had darkened perceptibly and the rock walls were even higher now, and for a time he seemed to regard them through a mist of rainbows.

Going back. A part of him still stood apart, but it seemed even smaller and farther away now. Parts of his life between childhood and now had become dreamlike, shimmering, and he had not noticed it happening. He began recalling seldom used names for things around him which he had thought long forgotten. The rain increased in intensity off to his right, though his way was still sheltered by the canyon wall. A trick of lightning seemed to show momentarily a reddish path stretching on before him.

"A *krel,* a *krel,*" he chanted as he walked, not knowing why. Free a cat to kill a Stragean, find a *krel* to kill a cat . . . What then? He chuckled. No answer to the odd vision. His mind played games with

145

the rock shapes around him. The Plains Indians had made more of a
cult out of the Rock people than his people had. But now it seemed
he could almost catch glimpses of the presence within the forms.
Who was that *bellicano* philosopher he had liked? Spinoza. Yes.
Everything alive, all of it connected, inside and out, all over. Very
Indian.

"Hah la tse kis!" he called out, and the echo came back to him.

The zigzag lightning danced above the high cliff's edge and when
its afterglow had faded he realized that night was coming on. He
increased his pace. He felt it would be good to be past Many Cherry
Canyon by the time full darkness fell.

The ground dropped away abruptly, and he made his way across a
bog, probing before him with his stick. He cleaned his boots then
before continuing. He ran a hand across the surface of a rock,
feeling its moist smoothnesses and roughnesses. Then he licked his
thumb and stared again into the shadowy places.

Moments came and went like dark tides among the stones as he
strode along, half-glimpsed images giving rise to free association,
racial and personal.

It seemed to sail toward him out of the encroaching darkness, its
prow cutting a V across his line of sight. It was Shiprock in
miniature, that outcrop ahead. As he swung along it grew larger and
it filled his mind. . . .

Irresistibly, he was thrown back. Again the sky was blue glass
above him. The wind was sharp and cold, the rocks rough, the going
progressively steeper. Soon it would be time to rope up. They were
approaching the near-vertical heights. . . .

He looked back at her, climbing steadily, her face flushed. She
was a good climber, had done it in many places. But this was
something special, a forbidden test. . . .

He gnashed his teeth and muttered, "Fool!"

They were climbing *tse bi dahi*, the rock with wings. The white
men called it Shiprock. It stood 7,178 feet in height and had only
been climbed once, some two hundred years earlier, and many had

146

died attempting the ascent. It was a sacred place, and it was now forbidden to climb upon it.

And Dora had liked climbing. True, she had never suggested this, but she had gone along with him. Yes, it had been his idea, not hers.

In his mind's eye, he saw their diminutive figures upon its face, reaching, hauling themselves higher, reaching. His idea. Tell him why. Tell Hastehogan, god of night, why—so that he may laugh and send a black wind out of the north to blow upon you.

Why?

He had wanted to show her that he did not fear the People's taboo, that he was better, wiser, more sophisticated than the People. He had wanted to show her that he was not really one of them in spirit, that he was free like her, that he was above such things, that he laughed at them. It did not occur to him until much later that such a thing did not matter to her, that he had been dancing a dance of fears for himself only, that she had never thought him inferior, that his action had been unnecessary, unwarranted, pathetic. But he had needed her. She was a new life in a new, frightening time, and—

When he heard her cry out he turned as rapidly as he could and reached out for her. Eight inches, perhaps, separated their fingertips. And then she was gone, falling. He saw her hit, several times.

Half blinded with tears, he had cursed the mountains and cursed the gods and cursed himself. It was over. He had nothing now. He was nothing. . . .

He cursed again, his eyes darting over the terrain to where, with a flick of its tail, he would have sworn a coyote had stood a moment ago, laughing, before it vanished into the shadows beyond the rise. Fragments of the chants from the old Coyoteway fire ritual came to him:

> *I will walk in the places where the black clouds come at me.*
> *I will walk in the places where the rain falls upon me.*
> *I will walk in the places where the lightning flashes at me.*
> *I will walk in the places where the dark fogs move about me.*

I will walk where the rainbows drift and the thunders roll.
Amid dew and pollen will I walk.
They are upon my feet. They are upon my legs. . . .

When he reached the spot where he thought he had seen the creature, he searched quickly in the dim light and thought that he detected a pawprint. Not important, though. It meant something. What, he could not say.

> *He is walking in the water. . . .*
> *On the trail beyond the mountains.*
> *The medicine is ready.*
> *. . . It is his water,*
> *a white coyote's water.*
> *The medicine is ready.*

As he passed Many Cherry Canyon he was certain that Cat was on his way. Let it be. This thing seemed destined, if not with Cat at his back then in some other fashion. Let it be. Things were looking different now. The world had been twisted slightly out of focus.

Dark, dark. But his eyes adjusted with unusual clarity. He would pass the cave of the Blue Bull. He would go on. He would take his rations as he walked. He would not rest. He would create another false way at Twin Trail Canyon. After that, he would obscure his passage even further. He would go on. He would walk in the water.

Come after me, Cat. The easy part is almost over.

Weak flash. The wind and the water swallow the thunder. He is laughing and his face is wet.

The black medicine lifts me in his hand. . . .

⟫⊢ *The Third Day* When the call came
through that Walter Sands was dead, having failed to respond to
treatment, Mercy Spender said a prayer, Fisher looked depressed
and Mancin looked out of the window. Ironbear poured a cup of
coffee, and for a long while no one said anything.

Finally, "I just want to go home," Fisher said.

"But we reached Singer," Elizabeth replied.

"If you want to call it that," he replied. "He's gone around the
bend. He's . . . somewhere else. His mind is running everything
through a filter of primitive symbolism. I can't understand him, and
I'm sure he can't understand me. He thinks he's deep under the
earth, traveling along some ancient path."

"He is," Ironbear said. "He is walking the way of the shaman."

Fisher snorted.

"What do you know about it?"

"Enough to understand some," he answered. "I got interested in
Indian things again when my father died. I even remembered some

149

stuff I'd forgotten for a long time. For all of his education and travels, Singer doesn't think in completely modern terms. In fact, he doesn't even think like a modern Indian. He grew up in almost the last possible period and place where someone could live in something close to a neolithic environment. So he's been to the stars. A part of him's always been back in those crazy canyons. And he was a shaman—a real one—once. He set out several days ago to go back to that part of himself, intentionally, because he thought it might help him. Now it's got hold of him, after all those years of repression, and it's coming back with a vengeance. That's what I think. I've been reading tapes on the Navajos ever since I learned about him, in all of my spare moments here. They're a lot different from other Indians, even from their neighbors. But they do have certain things in common with the rest of us—and the shaman's journey often goes underground when things are really tough."

" 'Us'? " Mancin said, smiling.

"Slip of the tongue," he answered.

"So you're saying this vicious alien beast is chasing a crazy Indian," Mercy stated. "And we just learned that the authorities won't go into those canyons after them because the place is too treacherous in the weather they're having. Sounds as if there's nothing we can do. Even if we coordinate as a group mind, the beast seems able to strike back at us pretty hard—and Singer can't understand us. Maybe we *should* go home and let them work it out between themselves."

"It would be different if there were something we could do," Fisher said, moving to stand beside Ironbear. "I'm beginning to see how you feel about the guy, but what the hell. If you're dead, lie down."

"We could attack the beast," Ironbear said softly.

"Too damned alien," Mancin said. "We don't have the key to his mind. He'd just slap us away like he did last time. Besides, this mass-mind business seems very risky. Not too much has really been done with it, and who knows how we might mess ourselves up? In any kind of cost-benefit analysis of it there's little to gain against unknown risks."

Ironbear rose to his feet and turned toward the door.

"Fuck your cost-benefit analysis," he said as he left the room.

Fisher started after him, but Elizabeth caught his eye.

"Let him go," she said. "He's too angry. You don't want a fight with a friend. There's nothing you can say to him now."

Fisher halted near the door.

"I couldn't reach him then, can't reach him now," he said. "I know he's mad, but . . . I don't know. I've got a feeling he could do something foolish."

"Like what?" Mancin asked.

"I don't know. That's just it. Maybe I'd better . . ."

"He'll brood for a while," Mancin said, "and then come back and try to talk us into something. Maybe we ought to agree to try to reach Singer and get him to head for some safe spot where he can be picked up. That might work."

"I've got a feeling it won't, but it's the best suggestion so far. How'll we know where a good spot is?"

Mancin thought for a time, then, "That friend of Singer's, the ranger," he said, "Yellowcloud. He'd know. Where's the printout with his number on it?"

"Ironbear had it," Elizabeth said.

"It's not on his chair. Not on the table either."

"You don't think . . . ?

Ironbear, wait! Elizabeth broadcast. *We're going to help! Come back!*

But there was no response.

They headed for the stair.

He was nowhere on the premises, and they guessed that he had tripped out from one of the downstairs boxes. They obtained the number from Information, but no one answered at Yellowcloud's place. It was not until half an hour later, while they were eating, that someone noticed that a burst-gun was missing from the guard room.

Roger Zelazny

PETROGRAFFITI

COYOTE STEALS VOICES FROM ALL LIVING THINGS

Nothing was capable of movement following Coyote's theft of sound from the world. Not until he was persuaded to call the Sun and Moon to life by giving a great shout and restoring noise to the land

NAYENEZGANI CONTINUES CIVIC IMPROVEMENT PLAN

At *Tse'a haildehe',* where a piece of rock brought up from the underworld was in the habit of drawing itself apart to form a pair of cliffs and closing again whenever travelers passed between, Nayenezgani today solved the problem by the ingenious use of a piece of elk's horn

2-RABBIT, 7-WIND. HOME TEAM SUCCESSFUL.

Quetzalcoatl, arriving this morning in Tula, was heard to remark, "Every man has his own rabbit." This was taken as a good sign by the local population, who responded with tortillas, flowers, incense, butterflies and snakes

Commercial traveler,
passing through

KIT CARSON GO HOME

I KILLED THREE DEER ACROSS THE WAY

BET THEY WERE LAME

SINGERS DO IT IN COLORED SANDS

FOUR APACHES KILLED A NAVAJO NEAR HERE

THAT'S HOW MANY
IT TAKES

SPIDER WOMAN DEMONSTRATES NEW ART

153

"I believe I'll call it textiles," she said, when questioned concerning

SOMEDAY VON DANIKEN WILL SAY
THIS IS AN ASTRONAUT

FORT SUMNER SUCKS

CHANGING WOMAN PUZZLED BY SONS' BEHAVIOR

"I suppose they get it from their father," she was heard to say, when told of the latest

BILLY BLACKHORSE SINGER AND HIS CHINDI PASSED THIS WAY
O-SINGER, O-CHINDI, AT END OF FIRST HALF

BLACK-GOD IS WATCHING

THE YELLOW MEDICINE LIFTS ME IN HIS HAND

WHEN IRONBEAR OCCURRED WITHIN the trip-box in Yellowcloud's home, the first thing to catch and hold his attention was a shotgun in the other man's hands, pointed at his midsection from a distance of approximately six feet.

"Drop that gun you're carrying," Yellowcloud said.

"Sure. Don't be nervous," Ironbear answered, letting the weapon fall. "Why are you pointing that thing at me?"

"Are you Indian?"

"Yes."

"Ha'át'íish biniinaa yíníya?"

Ironbear shook his head.

"I don't understand you."

"You're not Navajo."

"Never said I was. Matter of fact, I'm Sioux. Can't talk that either, though. Except maybe a few words."

"I'll say it in English: Why'd you come here?"

"I told you on the phone. I've got to find Singer—or the thing that's after him."

"I think maybe you're what's after him. It's easy to get rid of bodies around here, especially this time of year."

Ironbear felt his brow grow moist as he read the other man's thoughts.

"Hold on," he said. "I want to help the guy. But it's a long story and I don't know how much time we've got."

Yellowcloud motioned toward a chair with the barrel of his weapon.

"Have a seat. Roll up the rug first, though, and kick it out of the way. I'd hate to mess up a Two Gray Hills."

As he complied, Ironbear probed hard, trying to penetrate beyond the stream of consciousness. When he found what he was seeking, he

155

was not certain he could wrap his tongue around the syllables, but he tried.

"What did you say?" Yellowcloud asked, the weapon's barrel wavering slightly.

He repeated it, Yellowcloud's secret name.

"How'd you know that?" the other asked him.

"I read it in your mind. I'm a paranormal. That's how I got involved in this thing in the first place."

"Like a medicine man?"

"I suppose in the old days I would have been one. Anyway, there was a group of us and we were tracking the thing that's tracking Singer. Now the others want to quit, but I won't. That's why I want your help."

The rain continued as he talked. When the callbox buzzed, Yellowcloud switched it off. Later he got them coffee.

• • •

Running now, into the bowels of the earth, it seemed. Darker and darker. Soon he must slow his pace. The world had almost completely faded about him, save for the sounds—of wind, water, his drumming feet. Slow now. Yes. Now.

Ahead. Something in that stand of trees. Not moving. A light.

He advanced cautiously.

It appeared to be— But no. That was impossible. Yet. There it was. A trip-box. He was positive that it was against regulations to install one in the canyon.

He moved nearer. It certainly looked like a trip-box, there among the trees. He advanced and looked inside.

A strange one, though. No slot for the credit strip. No way to punch coordinates. He entered and studied it more closely. Just an odd red-and-white-flecked button. Without thinking, he moved his thumb forward and pushed it.

A mantle of rainbows swirled before his eyes and was gone. He looked inside. Nothing had changed. He had not been transported anywhere. Yet—

A pale light suffused the canyon now, as if a full moon hung overhead. But there was no moon.

He looked again at the box and for the first time saw the sign on its side. SPIRIT WORLD, it said. He shrugged and walked away from it. Save for the light, nothing seemed altered.

After some twenty paces, he turned and looked back. The box was gone. The stand of trees stood silvery to his rear, empty of any unnatural presence. To his right, the water gleamed in its rippling progress. The rain which fell into it seemed to be descending in slow motion, more a full-bodied mist than a downpour. And the next flash of lightning seemed a stylized inscription on the heavens.

Plainly marked before him now was the trail he must follow. He set his foot upon it and the wind chanted a staccato song of guidance as he went.

He moved quickly, approaching a bend in the canyon; more slowly then, as his slope steepened and narrowed. He dropped to a wider shelf as his way curved, hurried again as he followed it.

As he made the turn, he saw outlined to his right, ahead, a human figure standing on the opposite bank of the stream, at the very tip of a raised spit of land which projected out into the water. It was a man, and he seemed somehow familiar, and he had a kind of light about him which Billy found disturbing.

He slowed as he drew nearer, for the man was staring directly at him. For a moment, he was not certain how to address him, for he could not recall the circumstances of their acquaintance, and a meeting here struck him as peculiar. Then suddenly he remembered, but by then the other had already greeted him.

He halted and acknowledged the call.

"You are far from home," he said then, "from where I met you just the other day, in the mountains, herding sheep."

"Yes, I am," the other replied, "for I died that same evening."

A chill came across the back of Billy's neck.

"I did nothing to you," he said. "Why do you return to trouble me?"

157

"I have not returned to trouble you. In fact, I have not returned at all. It is you who have found your way to this place. That makes it different. I will do you no harm."

"I do not understand."

"I told you to follow a twisted way," the old singer said, "and I see that you have. Very twisted. That is good."

"Not entirely," Billy told him. "My *chindi* is still at my back."

"Your *chindi* turned right instead of left, following the false trail into Black Rock Canyon. You are still safe for a time."

"That's something, anyway," Billy said. "Maybe I can do it again."

"Perhaps. But what is it exactly that you are doing?"

"I am following a trail."

"And it brought you here. Do you think that we have met by accident?"

"I guess not. Do you know why we met?"

"I know only that I would like to teach you an old song of power."

"That's fine. I'll take all the help I can get," said Billy, glancing back along the way. "I hope it's not a real long one, though."

"It is not," the old singer told him. "Listen carefully now, for I can only sing it three times for you. To sing it four times is to make it work."

"Yes."

"Very well. Here is the song. . . ."

The old man began chanting a song of the calling of Ikne'etso, which Billy followed, understood and had learned by the third time he heard it. When the singer was finished he thanked him, and then asked, "When should I use this song?"

"You will know," the other answered. "Follow your twisted way now."

Billy bade him good-bye and continued along the northern slope. He considered looking back, but this time he did not do it. He trekked through the sparkling canyon and images of other worlds and of his life in cities rose and mingled with those about him until it seemed as if his entire life was being melted down and stirred

158

together here. But all of the associated feelings were also swirled together so that it was an emotional white noise which surrounded him.

He passed a crowd of standing stones and they all seemed to have faces, their mouths open, singing windsongs. They were all stationary, but at the far end of the group something came forward out of darkness.

It was a man, a very familiar man, who stood leaning against the last windsinger, smiling. He was garbed according to the latest fashion, his hair was styled, his hands well manicured.

"Hello, Billy," he said in English, and the voice was his own.

He saw then that the man was himself, as he could have been had he never come back to this place.

"That's right. I am your shadow," the other said. "I am the part of yourself you chose to neglect, to thrust aside when you elected to return to the blanket because you were afraid of being me."

"Would I have liked being you?"

The other shrugged.

"I think so. Time and chance, that's all. You and Dora would eventually have moved to a city after you'd proved to your own satisfaction how free you'd become. You took a chance and failed. If you'd succeeded you would have come this route. Time and chance. Eight inches of space. Such is the stuff lives are bent by."

"You are saying that if I'd proved how free I had become I still wouldn't really have been free?"

"What's free?" said the other, a faint green light beginning to play about his head. "To travel all good paths, I suppose. And you restricted yourself. I am a way that you did not go, an important way. I might have been a part of you, a saving part, but you slighted me in your pride that you knew best."

He smiled again, and Billy saw that he had grown fangs.

"I know you," Billy said then. "You are my *chindi*, my real *chindi*, aren't you?"

"And if I am," the other said, "and if you think me evil, you see me so for all of the wrong reasons. I am your negative self. Not

159

better, not worse, only unrealized. You summoned me a long time ago by running from a part of yourself. You cannot destroy a negation."

"Let's find out," Billy said, and he raised the laser snub-gun and triggered it.

The flash of light passed through his double with no visible effect.

"That is not the way to deal with me," said the other.

"Then the hell with you! Why should I deal with you at all?"

"Because I can destroy you."

"Then what are you waiting for?"

"I am not quite strong enough yet. So keep running, keep regressing into the primitive and I will grow in strength as you do. Then, when we meet again . . ." The other dropped suddenly to all fours and took on the semblance of Cat, single eye glistening, ". . . I will be your adversary by any name."

Billy drew the tazer and fired it. It vanished within the other's body, and the other became his double again and rose, lunging at him, the dart and cable falling to the ground and rewinding automatically.

Billy swung his left fist and it seemed to connect with something. His double fell back upon the ground. Billy turned and began running.

"Yes, flee. Give me strength," it called out after him.

When he looked back, Billy saw only a faint greenish glow near the place of the windsingers. He continued to hurry, until it vanished with another turning of the way. The voices of the windsingers faded. He slowed again.

The canyon widened once more; the stream was broader and flowed more slowly. He seemed to see distorted faces, both human and animal, within the water.

He had felt himself the object of scrutiny for some time now. But the feeling was growing stronger, and he cast about, seeking its source among fugitive forms amid shadow and water.

Cat?

No reply, which could mean anything. But no broadcast

apprehensions either—unless they came on only to be lost amid the emotional turbulence.

Cat? If it is you, let's have it out. Any time now. I'm ready whenever you are.

Then he passed a sharp projection of the canyon wall and he knew that it was not Cat whose presence he had felt. For now he beheld the strange entity which regarded him, and its appearance meshed with the sensation.

It looked like a giant totem pole. His people had never made totem poles. They were a thing of the people of the Northwest. Yet this one seemed somehow appropriate to the moment if incongruous to the place. It towered, and it bore four faces—and possibly a shadowy fifth, at the very top. There were the countenances of two women, one heavy-featured, one lean, and two men, one black and one white. And above them it seemed that a smiling masculine face hovered, smokelike. All of their eyes were fixed upon him, and he knew that he beheld no carving but a thing alive.

"Billy Blackhorse Singer," a neuter-gendered voice addressed him.

"I hear you," he replied.

"You must halt your journey here," it stated.

"Why?" he asked.

"Your mission has been accomplished. You have nothing to gain by further flight."

"Who are you?" he said.

"We are your guardian spirits. We wish to preserve you from your pursuer. Climb the wall here. Wait at the top. You will be met there after a time and borne to safety."

Billy's gaze shifted away from the spirit tower to regard the ground at his feet and the prospect before him.

"But I still see my trail out within this canyon," he said finally. "I should not depart it here."

"It is a false trail."

"No," he said. "This much I know: I must follow it to its end."

"That way lies death."

161

He was silent again for a time. Then, "Still must I follow it," he said. "Some things are more important than others. Even than death."

"What are these things? Why must you follow this trail?"

He took several deep breaths and continued to stare at the ground, as if considering it for the first time.

"I await myself at its ending," he said at last, "as I should be. If I do not follow this trail, it will be a different sort of death."

"Worse, I think," he added.

"We may not be able to help you if you go on."

"Then that is as it must be," he said. "Thank you for trying."

"We hear you," said the totem as it sank slowly into the ground, face by face sliding from view beneath stone, until only the final, shadowy one remained for an instant, smiling, it seemed, at him. "Gamble, then," it seemed to whisper, and then it, too, was gone.

He rubbed his eyes, but nothing changed. He went on.

> *. . . I walk on an invisible arch,*
> *feet ready to bear me anywhere.*

. . .

outcoming fra thplatz fwaters flwng awa thheadtopped tre andriving now to each where five now four apartapart horse on the mountain ghoti in thrivr selves towar bodystake like a longflwung water its several bays to go and places of ourown heads to sort sisters in the sky old men beneath the ground while coyote trail ahead blackbrid shadow overall and brotherone within the chalce of minds a partapartatrapatrap

"My God!" Elizabeth said, sinking back into her chair.

Alex Mancin poured a glass of water and drained it.

"Yes," said Fisher, massaging his temples.

Mercy Spender commenced a coughing spell which lasted for close to half a minute.

"Now what?" Fisher said softly.

Mancin shook his head.

162

"I don't know."

"Ironbear was right about his thinking he's in another world," Elizabeth said. "We're not going to move him."

"The hell with that," Fisher said. "We tried, and we got through, even if he did turn us into a totem. That's not what's bothering me, and you know it."

"He was there," Mercy said, "in the spirit."

"Somebody call the hospital and make sure Sands is really dead," Fisher said.

"I don't see how they could be mistaken, Charles," Elizabeth said. "But Mercy is right. He was with us, somehow, and it seems as if he's still somewhere near."

"Yes," Mercy put in. "He is here."

"You don't need the spirit hypothesis for what I think happened," Mancin finally stated.

"What do you mean?" Elizabeth asked.

"Just the memory of how he died. We were all of us together, functioning as that single entity of which we understand so little. I think that the trauma of his death served to produce something like a holograph of his mind within our greater consciousness. When we are apart like this it is weakened, but we all bear fainter versions, which is why we seem to have this sense of his presence. When we recreated the larger entity just now, the recombination of the traces was sufficient to reproduce a total functioning replica of his mind as it was."

"You see him as a special kind of memory when we are in that state?" Elizabeth asked. "Will it fade eventually, do you think?"

"Who can say?"

"So what do we do now?" Fisher asked.

"Check on Singer, I suppose, at regular intervals," Mancin said, "and renew the invitation to be picked up if he'll climb to some recognizable feature."

"He'll just keep refusing. You saw how fixed that mental set of his was."

"Probably—unless something happens to change it. You never

163

know. But I've been thinking about some of the things Ironbear said. He's owed the chance, and we seem the only ones who can give it to him."

"Okay by me. It seems harmless enough. Just don't ask me to go after that alien beast again. Once was enough."

"I'm not too anxious to touch it myself."

"What about Ironbear?"

"What about him?"

"Shouldn't we try to get in touch and let him know what we're doing?"

"What for? He's mad. He'll just shut us out. Let him call us when he's ready."

"I'd hate to see him do anything foolish."

"Like what?"

"Like go after that thing and find it."

Mancin nodded.

"Maybe you're right. I still don't think he'd listen, but—"

"He might listen to me," Fisher said, "but I'm not sure I can reach him myself at this distance."

"Why don't we locate the nearest trip-box to that canyon and go there?" Elizabeth said. "It will probably make everything easier."

"Aren't Indian reservations dry?" Mercy asked.

"Let's tell Tedders and get our stuff together. We'll meet back here in fifteen minutes," Fisher said.

"Walter thinks it's a good idea, too," Mercy said.

• • •

There is danger where I walk,
in my moccasins, leggings, shirt
of black obsidian.
My belt is a black arrowsnake.
Black snakes coil and rear about my head.
The zigzag lightning flashes from my feet,
my knees, my speaking tongue.
I wear a disk of pollen upon my head.
The snakes eat it.

There is danger where I walk.
I am become something frightful.
I am whirlwind and gray bear.
The lightning plays about me.
There is danger where I walk.

. . .

"I dropped him back here," Yellowcloud said, jabbing at the map, and Ironbear nodded, staring down at the outline of the long, sprawled canyons.

The rain, growing sleetlike, pelted against the floatcar in which they sat, parked near the canyon's rim. Reflexively, Ironbear raised the collar of his borrowed jacket. Pretty good fit. Lucky we're both the same size, he decided.

"I watched for a time," Yellowcloud continued, "to make sure he got down okay. He did, and I saw that he headed east then." His finger moved along the map and halted again. "Now, at this point," he went on, "he could have turned right into Black Rock Canyon or he could have kept on along Canyon del Muerto proper. What do you think?"

"Me? How should I know?"

"You're the witch-man. Can't you hold a stick over the map, or something like that, and tell?"

Ironbear studied the map more closely.

"Not exactly," he said. "I can feel him out there, down there. But a rock wall's just a rock wall to me, whether I'm seeing it through his eyes or my own. However . . ." He placed his finger on the map and moved it. "I'd guess he continued along del Muerto. He wanted lots of room, and Black Rock seems to dead-end too soon."

"Good, good. I feel he went that way, too. He chose a spot before it on purpose, I'd say. I'll bet the trail gets confused at the junction." Yellowcloud folded the map, turned off the interior light and started the engine. "Since we both agree," he said, turning the wheel, "I'll bet I can save us some time. I'll bet that if we head on up the rim, past that branch, and if we climb down into del Muerto, we'll pick up his trail along one of the walls."

165

"It'll be kind of dark."

"I've got goggles and dark-lights. Full spectrum, too."

"Can you figure out where he might be from where you dropped him and how fast he might be going?"

"Bet I can make a good guess. But we don't want to come down right on top of him now."

"Why not?"

"If something's after him, he's liable to shoot at anything he sees coming."

"You've got a point there."

"So we'll go down around Many Turkey Cave, Blue Bull Cave— right before the canyon widens. Should be easier to pick up the trail where it's narrow. Then we'll ignore any false signs leading into Twin Trail Canyon and start on after him."

Winds buffeted the small car as it made its way across a nearly trailless expanse, turning regularly to avoid boulders and dips which dropped too abruptly.

". . . Then I guess we just provide him with extra firepower."

"I'd like to try talking him out of it," Ironbear said.

Yellowcloud laughed.

"Sure. You do that," he said.

Ironbear scanned the other's thoughts, saw his impression of the man.

"Oh, well," he said. "At least I learned to shoot in the P-Patrol."

"You were P-Patrol? I almost joined that."

"Why didn't you?"

"Afraid I'd get claustrophobia in one of those beer cans in the sky. I like to be able to see a long way off."

They were silent for a time as they traveled through the blackness, dim shapes about them, snowflakes spinning in the headlight beams, changing back to rain, back to snowflakes again.

Then, "That thing that's after him," Yellowcloud said, "you say it's as smart as a man?"

"In its way, yeah. Maybe smarter."

166

"Billy may still have an edge, you know. He'll probably be mad to see us."

"That beast has chased him all over the world. It's built for killing, and it hates him."

"Even Kit Carson was afraid to go into these canyons after the Navajo. Had to starve us out in the dead of winter."

"Why was he scared?"

"The place was made for ambushes. Anyone who knows his way around down there could hold off a superior force, maybe slaughter it."

"This beast can read thoughts."

"So it reads that there's someone up ahead waiting to kill it. Doesn't have to be a mind reader to know that. And if it keeps following that's what could happen."

"It can change shape."

"It's still got to move in order to make progress. That makes it a target. Billy's armed now. It won't have it as easy as you seem to think."

"Then why'd you decide to come?"

"I don't like to see any outsider chasing Navajos on our land. And I couldn't let a Sioux have the first shot at the thing."

Without Yellowcloud, I wouldn't be worth much out here, Ironbear told himself. Even the little kids around here must know more than I do about getting around in this terrain, tracking, hunting, survival. I'm a damn fool for butting into this at all, physically. The only things I know about being an Indian come from Alaska, and that was a long time ago. So why am I here? I keep saying I like Singer, but why? Because he was some kind of a hero? I don't really think that's it. I think it's because he's an old-style Indian, and because my father might have been that way. At least I think of him that way. Could I be trying to pay off a debt of guilt here? It's possible, I guess. And all of my music had an Indian beat to it. . . .

The car slowed, worked its way into the shelter of a stone outcrop, came to a halt. The snow had turned back to rain, a slow, cold drizzle here.

"Are we there?" he asked.

"Almost," Yellowcloud replied. "There's an easy way down near here. Well, relatively easy. Let me get us some lights and I'll show you."

Outside, they donned small packs and slung their weapons. Yellowcloud shined his light toward the canyon.

"Follow me," he said. "There was a slide here a few years ago. Made a sort of trail. We'll be more sheltered once we reach the bottom."

Ironbear fell in behind him and they made their way to the rim of the canyon. Its floor was invisible, and the rocks immediately before him looked jagged and slippery. He said nothing, and shortly they began the descent, Yellowcloud playing his light before them.

As they climbed, the force of the rainfall lessened, until about halfway down they entered the full rainshadow of the wall and it ceased entirely. The rocks were drier and the pace of their descent increased. He listened to the wind and the noises of the rain.

Moving from rock to rock, he came, after a time, to wonder whether there was indeed a bottom. It began to seem as if they had been descending forever and that the rest of time would be a simple repetition of the grasping and lowering. Then he heard Yellowcloud call out, "Here we are!" and shortly thereafter he found himself standing on the canyon's floor, stony shapes distorted and flowing in the blacklight.

"Just stay put for a minute," Yellowcloud said. "I don't want any trails messed up." Then, "Can you use that trick of yours to tell whether there's anyone nearby?" he asked.

"There doesn't seem to be," Ironbear replied a few moments later.

"Okay. I'm going to use a normal light for a while here. Make yourself comfortable while I see what I can turn up."

Several minutes passed while Ironbear watched Yellowcloud's slowly moving light as the other man studied the ground, ranging farther and farther ahead, passing from left to right and back again.

Finally Yellowcloud halted. His figure straightened. He gestured for
Ironbear to come along, and then he began walking.

"Got something?" Ironbear asked, coming up beside him.

"He's been this way," he answered. "See?"

Ironbear nodded as he regarded the ground. He saw nothing, but
he read the recognition of signs within the other's mind.

"How long ago was he by here?"

"I can't say for sure. Doesn't really matter, though. Come on."

They hiked for nearly a quarter-hour in silence before Ironbear
thought to inquire, "Have you seen any signs of his pursuer?"

"None. A few dog tracks here and there are the only other things.
It couldn't be that size, from what you told me."

"No. It's got a lot more mass."

Yellowcloud ignored the false signs at Twin Trail Canyon and
continued along the northeasterly route of the main gap.

There was a hypnotic quality to the steady trudging, the unrolling
trail of rock, puddle, mud, shrub. The cold was not as bad as it might
have been with the wind softened as it was, but the numbness
Ironbear began to feel was more a mental thing. The waters splashed
and gurgled past. His arms swung and his feet strode in a near
mechanical fashion.

. . . Yes, yes, yes, yes, yes, yes, yes . . .

The wind seemed to be talking to him, seemed to have been
talking to him for a long while, lulling words, restful within the
routine of the movements.

. . . Lull, lull, lull, lull. Yes, rest, yes, rest, yest, yest, yest . . .

It was more than the wind and the rhythm, he suddenly knew.
There was someone—

Yes. Yes.

Power. Blackness. Death. It walked at his back. The thing. The
beast. It was coming.

Yes. Yes.

And there was nothing he could do about it. He could not even
slow his pace, let alone deviate from his course. It had him completely in its power, and so deftly had it taken control of him that he

169

had not even felt the insinuation of its presence. Until now, when it was far too late.

Yes. Yes, son of cities. You seem different from this other one, and both of you block my way. Keep walking. I will catch up with you soon. It will not matter then.

Ironbear tried again to turn aside, but his muscles refused to obey him. He was about to probe Yellowcloud's mind to see whether the other man had yet become aware of his condition. He held back, however. The creature somewhere to the rear was exerting a form of telepathic control over his nervous system. He could not tell whether it was also reading his thoughts. Perhaps. Perhaps not. He wanted to keep his own telepathic ability away from its awareness if he possibly could. Why, he was not certain. But he felt—

He heard a sound to the rear. A dislodged stone turning over, it seemed. He knew that if he did not break free in a few moments nothing that he felt would matter anymore. It would all be over for him. Everything. The beast Singer called Cat was almost upon him.

His feet continued their slow, steady movements. He tried to visualize Cat, but he could not. A malevolent shadow with sinuous movements . . . a large eye drifting like a moon . . . The images came and departed. None seemed adequate for the approaching beast—powerful, fearless . . .

Fearless?

An image leaped to mind, a question keeping it company: How strong a mental impression could he project? Fisher could create solid-seeming illusions with ease. Could he manage with a fraction of that verisimilitude if he backed it with everything he had? Perhaps just enough to disconcert?

There was no real pause, though, between the idea and the effort. The speculation ran simultaneous with the attempt, habit of the reflective part of himself.

The sandy stretch across which he had just passed . . . He projected the image of its eruption, with the shining triangular form bursting upward, lunging forward, reaching to embrace his pursuer. . . .

Krel! Krel! he sent, concentrating to achieve perfection in its display.

He halted, feeling the panic waves from behind him, aware of controlling his own movements once more, aware, too, that Yellowcloud had halted.

Krel! But even as he reinforced the image with every feeling of menace and terror with which he found himself freshly familiar, even as he unslung the burst-gun and fitted his hand to its grip, he realized that while his movements were now his own he was afraid to execute the necessary turn to face the thing which stood behind him.

The report of Yellowcloud's weapon shattered his paralysis. He spun about, the burst-gun at ready.

Cat, in the light of Yellowcloud's beam, was dropping to the ground from an erect posture, and that awful eye seemed fixed upon his own, burning, boring.

He triggered his weapon, moving it, and dirt and gravel blew backward from a line traced on the ground in front of the beast.

Yellowcloud fired again and Cat jerked as he plunged forward. Ironbear raised the muzzle of his own weapon and triggered another burst. It stitched a wavering line along Cat's neck and shoulder.

And then everything went silent and black as he felt the impact of Cat's body upon his own.

· · ·

They sat or lay in their rooms at the Thunderbird Lodge, not far from the mouths of the canyons. It was as if they were all together in one room, however, for the walls did not impede their conversation.

Well? Elizabeth asked. *What have you learned?*

I'm going to try again, Fisher answered. *Wait a few minutes.*

You've been at it for quite a while, Mancin said.

Sometimes there are snags—unusual states of mind that are hard to pick up. You know.

Something's wrong, Mancin said. *I've been trying, too.*

Maybe we're too late, Mercy put in.

Don't be ridiculous!

171

I'm just trying to be realistic.

I got through to Yellowcloud's house while you were trying for contact, Elizabeth said. *His wife told me that he and Ironbear left together some time ago. They went over to the canyon, she said.*

After Singer? Mancin asked.

She wouldn't say any more about it. But why else?

Indeed.

I'm going to try again now, Fisher said.

Wait, Elizabeth told him.

Why?

You're not getting anywhere by yourself.

You mean we should get together again and try?

Why not? That is why we're here. To work together.

Do you think Sands . . . ? Mancin began.

Probably, Elizabeth said.

Yes, Mercy said. *But he wouldn't hurt us.*

Well, you're right about why we're here, Mancin said to Elizabeth.

And if we can't locate Jimmy? Fisher said. *What then?*

Try again with Singer, Elizabeth said. *Perhaps this time he'll listen.*

• • •

Now you travel your own trail, alone.

What you have become, we do not know.

What your clan is now, we do not know.

Now, now on, now, you are something not of this world.

• • •

Walking. Through the silver and black landscape. Slow here. Confuse the way. As if for an ambush from behind those rocks. Erase the next hundred feet or so with a branch of shrubbery. Good. Go on. The way is clear. Vaguely red-and-white flecked. Walking. Skyflash mirrored in waters twisting. Faint drumbeat once again. Consistency of windsound within the slant of walls. Small spray glassmasking face here, eyelash prisms spectrumbreaking rainbows geometric dance of lights. Wipe. Shadows leapback. Coyotedog smile fading between the light and the dark. Cross here, splashing. Wherever trail runs follow the feet. Around. Over. Masked dancers within the shadows, silent. Far, far to the rear, a faint green light. Why look back? To turn is to embrace. Climb now. Descend again. It narrows soon, then widens again. A thing with many eyes sits upon a high ledge but does not stir. Frozen, perhaps, or only watching. Louder now the drumbeat. Moving to its rhythms. Fire within the heart of a stone. Rain *yei* bending, bridgelike, from above to below. Birdtracks behind a mooncurved wall. Thighbone of horse. Empty hogan. Half-burned log. Touch the mica that glistens like pollen. Remember the song the old man—

. . . Singer.

Faint, faint. The wind or its echo. Tired word of tired breath. *Billy Blackhorse . . .*

Across again now, to that rocky place.

I feel you—up there, somewhere—tracker . . .

Something. Something he should remember. This journey. To follow his trail. But.

Your friends did not stop me. I am still coming, hunter.

Ghost of the echo of the wind. Words in his head. Old friends, perhaps. Someone known.

Why do you not answer me? To talk gives nothing away.

Ghost-cat, *chindi*-thing. Yes. Cat.

I am here, Cat.

And I follow you.

I know.

It is a good place you have chosen.

It chose me.

Either way. Better than cities.

Billy paused to muddle his trail, create the impression of another possible ambush point.

. . . Coming. You cannot run forever.

Only so far as I must. You are hurt . . .

Yes. But not enough to stop me. We will meet.

We will.

I feel you are stronger here than you were before.

Perhaps.

Whichever of us wins, it is better this way than any other. We are each of us the last of our kind. What else is there for us?

I do not know.

It is a strange country. I do not understand everything about it.

Nor do I.

Soon we will meet, old enemy. Are you glad that you ran?

Billy tried hard to think about it.

Yes, he finally said.

Billy thought of the song but knew that it was not the time to sing it. Thunder mumbled down the canyon.

You have changed, hunter, since last we were this close.

I know where I'm going now, Cat.

Hurry then. I may be closer than you think.

Watch the shadows. You may even be nearer than you *think.*

Silence. The big widening and a clear view far ahead. He halted, puzzled, suddenly able to see for a great distance. Like a ribbon, his trail led on and on and then wound upward. He did not understand, but it did not matter. He broke into his ground-eating jog. In the darkness high overhead, he heard the cry of a bird.

Farther yet, he returns with me, Nayenezgani,
spinning his dark staff for protection.
The lightnings flash behind him and before him.
To the ladder's first rung,
to the Emergence Place
he returns with me;
and the rainbow returns with me
and the talking ketahn *teaches me.*
We mount the ladder's twelve rungs.

174

Small blue birds sing above me,
Cornbeetle sings behind me.
Hashje-altye *returns with me.*
I will climb Emergence Mountain,
Chief Mountain, Rain Mountain,
Corn Mountain, Pollen Mountain. . . .
Returning. Upon the pollen figure to sit.
To own the home, the fire, the food,
the resting place, the feet, the legs, the body,
to hold the mind and the voice, the power
of movement. The speech, that is blessed.
Returning with me. Gathering these things,
Climbing. Through the mists and clouds,
the mosses and grasses,
the woods and rocks, the earth,
of the four colors. Returning.
"Grandchild, we stand upon the rainbow."

Running. THE WIND AND WATER-
sounds now a part of the drumbeat. Path grown clearer and clearer.
Blood-red now and dusted as with ice flakes.

The ground seemed to shake once, and something like a tower of smoke rose before him in a twisting at the side of the trail. Changing colors, the pillar braided itself as it climbed, and five shifting faces took form within it. He recognized his guardian spirits.

"Billy, we have come to ask you again," they said in a single voice. "The danger increases. You must leave the trail, leave the canyon. Quickly. You must go to a place where you will be met and taken to safety."

"I cannot leave the trail now," he answered. "It is too late to do that. My enemy approaches. My way is clear before me. Thank you again. There is no longer a choice for me in this."

"There is always a choice."

"Then I have already made it."

The smoke-being blew apart as he passed it.

He saw what appeared to be the end of the trail now, and a small atavistic fear touched him as he realized where it would take him. It was to the Mummy Cave, an old place of the dead, that it ran, high up the canyon wall.

As he advanced, it seemed to grow before him, a ruin within a high alcove. A green light played behind one of the windows for an eyeblink and a half. And then the wind was muffled, and then it rose again. And again. Again.

Now the sound came like the flapping of a giant piece of canvas high in the sky. He kept his eyes upon his goal and continued to follow his trail toward the foot of the wall. And as he ran the sound grew louder, felt nearer. Finally it seemed directly overhead, and he sensed each beat upon his body. Then a dark shape moved past, through the upper air.

When he raised his eyes he beheld an enormous bird-form dipping to settle atop the cliff wall high above the place of the Mummy Cave. He slowed as he neared the foot of the wall and encountered the talus slope. And he knew as he beheld the dark thing, settling now and staring downward, that he beheld Haasch'ééshzhiní, Black-god, master of the hunt. He looked away quickly, but not before he met the merciless stare of a yellow eye fixed upon him.

Must I end this thing beneath your gaze, Dark One? he wondered. For I am both the hunter and the hunted. Which side does that put you on?

He mounted the slope, his eyes now following the trail gone vertical up toward the recessed ruin. Yes, that did seem the easiest route. . . .

He approached the wall, took the first foothold and handhold and commenced climbing.

Climbing. Slowly over the more slippery places. A strange tingling in the palms of the hands as he mounted higher. Like the time—

No. He halted. Everything he was was a part of the hunt. But it was also a part of the past. Let it go. Climb. Hunt. Position is what is important. That lesson comes with memory. Achieve it now. He drew himself higher, not looking at the dark shadow far above, not looking back. Soon.

Soon he would enter the place of death and await his pursuer. The running should be nearing its end. Hurry. Important to be up there and out of sight when Cat enters the area. Wet handhold. Grip tightly.

Glance upward. Yes. In sight now. Soon. Careful. Pull. There.

After several minutes, he drew himself up onto a ledge, moved to the left. Another hold. Up again.

Half crawling. Okay now. Rise again. Move toward the wall. Enter. No green light. Over the wall . . .

He passed along the rear of the wall, peering through gaps out over the floor of the canyon. Nothing. Nothing yet in sight. Keep going. That large opening . . .

All right. Halt. Unsling the weapon. Check it out. Rest it on the ledge. Wait.

Nothing. Still nothing. The place was damp and filled with rubble. He ran his eyes across the open spaces before him, the entire prospect palely illuminated through screens of phosphorescent mist. But waiting was a thing at which he excelled. He settled with his back against a block of stone, his eyes upon the canyon, one hand upon the weapon.

Nearly an hour passed with no changes in the scene before him.

And then a shadow, slow, inching along the wall, far to his left and ahead. Its creeping barely registered, until at some point he realized that there was nothing to cast it.

He raised the weapon—it had a simple sight—and zeroed it in on the shadow. Then he thought about the accuracy of the thing and lowered it again. Too far. If the shadow were really Cat he did not want to take a chance on missing and giving away his position.

It stopped. It flowed into the form of a rock and remained stationary for a long while. He could almost believe that the entire sequence had been a trick of light and shadow. Almost. He drew a bead on the rock and held it there.

You are somewhere near, Billy. I can feel you.

He did not respond.

Wherever you are, I will be there shortly.

Should he risk a shot after all? he wondered. It would take Cat a while to assume a more mobile shape. He would doubtless have several opportunities during that time. . . .

Movement again. The rock shifted, flowed, reformed farther along the wall.

Suffer, tracker. You are going to die. Your first shot will betray you and I will dodge all of the successive ones. You will see me when I am ready to be seen and you will fire it then.

The movement commenced again, drifting toward a real rock beneath a shelflike overhang. Within the amorphous form the glittering of Cat's eye became visible; his limbs began to take form.

Billy bit his lip, recalling having seen a torglind metamorph run up a near-vertical wall on the home planet. He triggered the weapon then and missed.

Cat froze for a split second as the flash occurred high overhead, then moved more slowly than Billy had anticipated, leading Billy to believe that the beast was indeed injured. Cat sprang back toward a line of stones nearer the wall. And then, realizing his mistake as he glanced upward, his legs bunched beneath him and he sprang forward again. But not in time.

A large slab of stone facing, blasted loose by the shot, slid down the wall, striking the shelf beneath which Cat crouched. Even as his feet left the ground, it descended upon him.

Hunter! I believe—you've won. . . .

Billy fired again. This time he scorched the earth ten yards off to

178

the right of the fall. He moved the barrel slightly to the left and triggered the weapon again. This time the top of the rubble heap exploded.

It seemed that he could make out a single, massive forelimb projected near the front of the pile. But at that distance he could not be certain.

Was that a twitch?

He fired again, blasting the center of the heap.

The canyon rang with a massive cawing note. The flapping sound began again, slowly. He looked up briefly and glimpsed the shadow moving off to his right.

"It is over," he sang, head rested upon his forearm, "and my thanks rise like smoke. . . ."

His words trailed off as his eyes moved across the canyon floor. Then his brow furrowed. He raised himself. He leaned forward to peer.

"Why?" he said aloud.

But nothing answered.

The trail he had followed did not terminate at this place. Somehow he had not noticed this earlier. It ran off to his right, curving out of sight beyond the canyon wall, presumably continuing on into the farther reaches of the place.

He slung his weapon and adjusted his pack. He did not understand, but he would go on.

He returned to the place where he had climbed and began his descent.

• • •

His shoulder ached. Also, it was raining on his face and a sharp stone was poking him in the back. He was aware of these things for some time before he realized that they meant he was alive.

Ironbear opened his eyes. Yellowcloud's light lay upon the ground nearby, casting illumination along a gravel slope.

He turned his head and saw Yellowcloud. The man was seated with his back against a stone, legs straight out before him. Both of his hands were gripping his left thigh.

179

Ironbear raised his head, reached out a hand, levered himself upward.

"I live," he said, swinging into a sitting position. "How're you?"

"Broken leg," Yellowcloud answered. "Above the knee."

Ironbear rose, crossed to the light and picked it up, turned back toward Yellowcloud.

"Bad place for a break," he said, advancing. "Can't even hobble."

He squatted beside the other man.

"I'm not sure what's the best thing to do," he said. "Got any suggestions?"

"I've already called for help. My portaphone wasn't damaged. They'll be along with a medic. Get me out of here in a sling if they have to. Don't worry. I'll be okay."

"Why are we still alive?"

"It didn't think we were worth killing, I guess. Just an annoyance, to be brushed aside."

"Makes you feel real important, doesn't it?"

"I'm not complaining. Listen, there's dry wood along the wall. Get me a couple of armloads, will you? I want a fire."

"Sure." He moved to comply. "I wonder how far along that thing has gotten?"

"Can't you tell?"

"I don't want to get near it at that level. It can hurt you just with its mind."

"You going after it?"

"If I can figure a way to follow it."

Yellowcloud smiled and turned his head, gesturing with his chin.

"It went that way."

"I'm not a tracker like you."

"Hell, you don't have to be. That thing's heavy and it's running, right out in the open. Nothing fancy. It couldn't care less whether one of us knows where it went. You take the light. I'll have the fire. You'll be able to see the marks it left."

He carried over the first load of kindling, went back to look for more. By the time he returned with the second load, Yellowcloud had a fire going.

"Anything else I can do for you?" he asked.

"No. Just get moving."

He slung his weapon and picked up the light. When he played the beam up the canyon he saw the tracks readily enough.

"And take this." Yellowcloud passed him the portaphone.

"Okay. I'll go try again."

"Maybe you ought to aim for its eye."

"Maybe I should. See you."

"Good luck."

He turned and began walking. The water was a dark, speaking thing whose language he did not understand. The way was clear. The tracks were large.

• • •

> *The wind stirs the grasses.*
> *The snow glides across the earth.*
> *The whirlwind walks on the mountain,*
> *raising dust.*
> > *The rocks are ringing*
>
> *high on the mountain, behind the fog.*
> *The sun's light is running out*
> *like water from a cracked pitcher.*
> *We shall live again.*
> *The snowy earth*
> *slides out of the whirling wind.*
> *We shall live again.*

AROUND THE CURVE OF THE CANYON wall, walking. Gusts of wind here over stream grown wider, swirling glittering particles across watersong gone wild. Other side more sheltered but the red way lies close to the wall, here, rising now. Ripples like rushing pictographs. Pawprints of the perfidious one. Ice-rimed bones beside the trail. Rabbit. Burnt hogan, green glow within. Place of death. Shift eyes. Hurry on. Shine of crystal. Snow-streaked wall, texture of feathers. Trail winding on. As far as the eye will go. What now the quarry?

Pause to drink at the crossing of tributary streamlet. Burning cold, flavored of rock and earth. Fog bank ahead, moving toward him, masked dancers within, about a south-blue blaze. Rhythms in the earth. He is become a smoke, drifting along his way, silent and featureless, rushing to merge with that place of flux and earthdance cadence. Yes, and be lost in it.

White and soft, smothering sounds, like that place where he had hunted the garlett, so long ago . . .

Dancers to the right, dancers to the left, dancers crossing his way. Do they even see him, invisible and spiritlike, passing among them, along the stillbright, stillred way written upon the ground as with fire and blood?

One draws nearer bearing something covered by a cloth woven with an old design. He halts, for the dancer moves to bar his way, thrusting the thing before him. It is uncovered, displaying a pair of hands. He stares at them. That scar near the base of the left thumb . . . They are his hands.

At the recognition they rise to hover in front of him, as if he were holding them before his face. He feels them, glovelike, at the extremity of his spirit. He had skinned game with them, fought with them, stroked Dora's hair with them. . . .

He lets them fall to his sides. It is good to have them back again.

182

The dancer moves away. Billy swirls like a whirlwind of snow and continues along his trail.

There is no time. A cluster of gray sticks, rising from the earth on the slope to his right, beside the trail . . . He pauses to watch as the sticks turn green, bumps appearing along their surfaces to become buds. The buds crack, leaves unwind themselves, turn, enlarge. White flowers come forth.

He passes, swinging his hands. Another dancer with another parcel approaches from his left.

He halts, hovering, and with his hands he accepts the gift of his feet and restores them to their places on the ground below him. The many miles we have come together . . .

Walking, again walking, upon the trail. Feeling the heartbeat of the earth through the soles of his feet. There is no time. Snowflakes blow upward before him. The stream has reversed its direction. Blood flows back into the wounded deer lying still across his way. It springs to its hoofs, turns and is gone.

Now, like curtains, a parting of the fog. Four masked dancers advance upon him, bearing the body that is his own. When he wears it again, he thanks them, but they withdraw in silence.

He moves on along the trail. The fog is shifting. Everything is shifting but the trail.

He hears a sound which he has not heard in a great counting of years. It begins off in the distance behind him and rises in pitch as it comes on: the whistle of a train.

Then he hears the chugging. They no longer make engines of this sort. There is nothing here for it to run on. There is—

He sees the rails paralleling his trail. That ledge ahead seems a platform now. . . .

The whistle sounds again. Nearer. He feels the throb of the thing, superimposed upon the earth rhythms. A train such as he has not beheld in years is coming. Coming, impossibly, through this impossible place. He keeps walking, as the sound of it fills the world. It should be rushing up beside him at any moment.

The shriek of the whistle fills his hearing. He turns his head.

Yes, it has come. An ancient, black, smoke-puffing dragon of an engine, a number of passenger cars trailing behind. He hears the screaming of its brakes begin.

He looks back to the area of the platform, to where a single, slouched figure now stands waiting. Almost familiar . . .

With a clattering and the cries of metal friction the engine draws abreast of him, slowing, slowing, and passes to halt beside the platform. He smells smoke and grease and hot metal.

The figure on the platform moves toward the first passenger car, and he now recognizes the old dead singer who had taught him the song. Just before boarding the man turns and waves to him.

His gaze slides back along the coach's windows. Behind every one is a face. He recognizes all of them. They are all people he has known who are now dead—his mother, his grandmother, his uncles, his cousins, two sisters . . .

Dora.

Dora is the only one who is looking at him. The others stare past, talking with one another, regarding the landscape, the new passenger. . . .

Dora is looking directly at him, and her hands are working with the latches at the lower corners of the window. Almost frantically, she is pushing and lifting.

The whistle blows again. The engine surges. He finds himself running, running toward the train, the car, the window. . . .

The train jerks, rattles. The wheels turn.

Dora is still working at the latches. Suddenly the window slides upward. Her mouth is moving. She is shouting, but her words are lost among the noises of the train.

He shouts back. Her name. She is leaning forward out of the window now, right arm extended.

The train is picking up speed, but he is almost beside it. He reaches. Their hands are perhaps a meter apart. Her lips are still moving, but he cannot hear her words. For a moment his vision swims, and it is as if she were falling away from him.

He increases his pace and the distance between their hands narrows—two feet, a foot, eight inches. . . .

Their hands clasp, and she smiles. He matches the train's velocity for a moment before the tension begins. Then he realizes that he must let go.

He opens his hand and watches her rush away. He falls.

How long he lies there he does not know. When he looks again, the train is gone. There are no tracks. There is no platform. His outstretched arm lies within the icy stream. Snow is falling upon him. He rises.

The big flakes drift by. The wind has died. The water sounds are muted. He raises his hand and stares at it like a new and unfamiliar thing within the silence.

After a long while, he turns and seeks the trail again. He continues his journey along it.

Trudging. Alternating elation and depression, finally all mixed together. To have caught her and then had to let her go. To ride Smohalla's ghost-train through the snow. Another breaking apart. Would there be a putting together again?

He realized then that he was traversing an enormous sand-painting. All of the ground about him was laid out in stylized, multicolored fashion. He walked in the footprints of the rainbow, passing between *Eth-hay-nah-ashi*—Those-who-go-together. They were the twins created in the Second world by Begochiddy. First Man and the others had come up from the Underworld along this route. The painting itself was one used in *Hozhoni,* the Blessingway. His trail followed the rainbow to the cornstalk, where it changed to the yellow of corn pollen. Upward, upward along the stalk then. The sky was illuminated by a brilliant flash as he passed alongside the female rainbow and the male lightning. Passing between the figures of Big Fly, heading north to the yellow pollen footsteps.

Emerge to take up the trail again, passing the mouth of the large canyon to the right, continuing northward. Alone, singing. There was beauty in the falling snow. Beauty all around him . . .

185

Admire it while you may, tracker.

Cat! You're dead! It is over between us!

Am I, now?

I touched your limb at the place where you fell. It was stiff and glassy. There was no life in you.

Have it your way.

Nor could anything have gotten out from beneath that heap of stone.

You've convinced me. I will go back and lie down.

Billy looked backward, saw nothing but snowfall within the canyon.

. . . But I'll find you first.

That shouldn't be too hard.

I am glad to hear you say that.

I like to finish what I start. Hurry.

Why don't you wait for me?

I've a trail to follow.

And that is more important than me?

You? You are nothing now.

That is not too flattering. But very well. If we must meet upon your trail again, we will meet upon your trail.

Billy checked his weapons.

You should have taken the train, he said.

I do not understand you, but it does not matter.

But it does, Billy said, rounding another rock and seeing the trail go on.

A whirlwind of snow danced across the water. He heard the thump of a single drumbeat.

. . . The blue medicine lifts me in his hand.

THE PAIN IN HIS SHOULDER HAD
subsided to a dull throbbing. He peered into pockets of shadow as
he passed them, wondering whether the beast might be waiting to
spring upon him, knowing the fear to be irrational since the tracks
lay clear before him—and why should it go to the trouble of
doubling back to lay in wait for him when it could have taken an
extra second to smash him in passing back when they had met?

Ironbear cursed, still looking. His breath emerged as plumes of
steam before him. His nose was cold and his eyes watered
periodically.

Yellowcloud had been right. There was no problem at all in
following this trail. Simple and direct. Deep and clear cut.

Was that a movement to the left?

Yes. The wind stirring bushes.

He cursed again. Had his ancestors really led war parties? So
much for genetics . . .

Jimmy. Don't shut me out!

I won't, Charles. I can use the company.

Where are you? What's happening?

I'm in the canyon, following the thing.

*We're here in Arizona, at the hotel near to where the canyons start.
Why?*

*To help, if we can. You're following the beast? Is Yellowcloud with
you?*

He was, but it broke his leg. He's sent for help.

You've met it?

*Yeah. Got a sprained shoulder out of the deal. Put a few shots into
the thing, though.*

Were you unconscious?

Yes.

I wondered why I couldn't reach you for a while there. Have you been in touch with Singer?

No.

We have. That's one crazy Indian.

I think he knows what he's doing.

Do you know what you're doing?

Being another crazy Indian, I guess.

I'd say.

Looks like we cross the water here.

I think you ought to get out. That's two trails you're following, not one.

It's starting to snow now. God, I hope it doesn't cover the tracks. Melting when it hits, though. That's good.

Sounds as if that thing almost killed you once.

They're changing shape.

The tracks?

Yeah, and moving nearer the wall. Wonder what that means?

It means you'd better shoot at anything that moves.

Something wet and glassy here . . . Wonder what its blood looks like?

How far along are you, anyway?

Don't know. My watch is broken. Seems as if I've been walking forever.

Maybe you'd better stop and rest.

Hell, no. It's time to try jogging for a while. I've got a feeling. I think I'm near and I think it's hurt.

I don't want to be in your mind if it gets you.

Don't go yet. I'm scared.

I'll wait.

For the next quarter-hour he felt Fisher's silent presence as he ran beside the pleated wall. They did not converse again until he slowed to catch his breath near a turning place.

It's going slow here, sneaking. But there's only a little of that glassy stuff, he observed.

You go slow.

I am. I'll just switch to the blacklight and put on the goggles. I'll get down low and look around the corner.

There was a long silence.

Well?

I don't see anything.

He turned the light toward the ground.

The trail's changing again. I'm going to follow it.

Wait. Why don't you probe?

I'm afraid to touch its mind.

I'd be a lot more afraid of the rest of it. Why not just take it very slow and easy? Just scan for its presence. Sneak up mentally. I'll help.

You're right, but I'll do it myself.

He reached out into the pocket canyon before him. Gingerly at first. Then with increased effort.

Not there. Nothing there, he said. *I see the trail, but I don't feel the beast. Singer either, for that matter. They must have gone on.*

It would seem . . .

He neared the corner, walking slowly, observing the markings on the ground. The markings were altered beyond the turning, forming a troughlike line. They narrowed, widened, halted in the form of circular depressions.

He paused when he saw where they led, rushed forward when he saw something other than rock.

Singer's prints marked the ground before the rough cairn, near to the protruding limb. It was a longer while before he could bring himself to move a few stones and then only after probing thoroughly. He kept at it for several minutes, until he was sweating and breathing heavily. But at last he beheld the eye, dull now, in the sleek, unmoving head.

He got it, Fisher said. *He nailed the thing.*

Ironbear did not respond.

It's over, Fisher told him. *Singer won.*

He's beautiful, Ironbear said. *That neck . . . the eye, like a jewel . . .*

Dead, Fisher said. *Wait while I check. I'll tell you where to climb out. We'll have someone pick you up.*

189

But where's Singer?

*I guess he knows how to take care of himself. He's safe now. He'll
turn up when he's ready. Hang on.*

I'm going after him.

What? What for?

*I don't know. Call it a feeling. Say I just want to see the man after
all this.*

How'll you find him?

*I'm starting to get the hang of this tracking business. I don't think it
will be too hard.*

It's all over—and that's a dangerous place.

*His trail has run through safe spots so far. Besides, I've got a phone
here.*

Don't you flip out, too!

Don't worry about it.

Ironbear turned away, pushed up his goggles, shifted to normal
spectrum, began following Singer's tracks.

I'm going to leave you for a time, Fisher said. *I'm going to tell the
others. Also, I've got to rest.*

Go ahead.

Ironbear headed north. For a moment it seemed that he heard a
train whistle, and he thought of his father. Fat snowflakes filled the
air. He wrapped his muffler around his nose and mouth and kept
going.

Mercy Spender

when she heard the news,
opened the bottle of gin she had brought along

& poured herself a stiff one,
humming "Rock of Ages" all the while;
feeling responsibility dissolve,
giving thanks,
deciding which books to read
& what to knit
during her convalescence;
offered a word or two
for the soul of Walter Sands,
whom she saw before her
in the glass,
suddenly,
shaking his head;
"Rest in peace," she said
& chugged it,
& when she went to pour another
the glass broke somehow
& she was very sleepy
& decided to turn in
& save the serious part
for tomorrow;
& her sleep was troubled.

Alex Mancin

tripped home when he heard the news,
the game being over,
his side having won
again;

& after he'd said good-bye to the others
& gone through,
he visited the kennels
& played with the dogs for a time,
lithe, yipping & licking—
he could read their affection for him
& it warmed him—
& then visited his console,
a glass of warm milk at his right hand,
taking action on the multitude of messages
which had come in,
as always;
too keyed up to sleep,
thoughts of the recent enterprise
dashing into and out of his mind
like puppies;
& the smile of Walter Sands
seemed to flash for a moment
on the screen
as he read a list of stock quotations
& toyed with a pair of souvenir dice
he'd found in the bottom drawer
of the dresser in the back room.

Elizabeth Brooke

wanted to get laid,
was surprised
at the intensity of the feeling,

but realized that the previous days'
pace & tensions, suddenly relaxed,
called for some physical release, too;
& so she bade the others farewell
& tripped back to England
to call her friend to join her
for tea,
to talk of her recent experiences,
listen to some chamber music
& lay the ghost of Walter Sands
which had been troubling her
more than a little.

Charles Dickens Fisher

in his room at the Thunderbird Lodge
with a pot of coffee,
looked out of the window at the snow,
thinking about his brother-in-law
& the Indians
in western movies he had seen
& wilderness survival
& the great dead beast
whose image he caused to appear
before him on the lawn
(frightening a couple across the way
who happened to look out
at that moment),
recalled from a video picture

he had summoned earlier,
eye blazing like Waterford crystal,
fangs like stalactites;
& then he banished it
& produced a full-sized
image of Walter Sands,
sitting in the armchair
looking back at him,
& when he asked him,
"How do you like being dead?"
Sands shrugged
& replied,
"It has its benefits,
it has its drawbacks."

Going. ALONG THE WESTERN RIM OF
the canyon now, heading into the northeast. Turning, taking an even
more northerly route. Away from the canyon, across the snows,
toward the trees. His way had brought him over the water and up
the wall nearly an hour before. Up here where the wind was strong,
though the snowfall had lessened to an occasional racing flake.

He bore on. A coyote howled somewhere in the trees or beyond
them, ahead. A woodland smell came to him as he advanced, and
the sounds of rattling branches.

He looked back once before he entered the wood. It seemed that
there was a greenish glow rising just above the rim of the canyon. He
lost sight of it in a snowswirl a moment later, and then there were
trees all around him and a diminishment of the wind. Ice fell with
crisp and glassy sounds when he brushed against boughs. It was like

another place, a place of perpetual twilight and cold, where he had hunted what he came to call the ice bears, the sun a tiny, pale thing creeping along the horizon. At any moment the high-pitched whistle of the bears might come to him, and then he would have only moments in which to throw up the barrier and lay down a paralytic fire before the pack swirled in toward him. Move the barrier then to preserve the fallen before their fellows devoured them. Call for the shuttle ship. . . .

He glanced overhead, half expecting to see it descending now. But there was only a pearl-gray folding of clouds in every direction. This hunt was different. The thing he sought would not be taken so simply, nor borne away for enclosure. All the more interesting.

He crossed an ice-edged streamlet and his way swerved abruptly, following its course through an arroyo where something with green eyes regarded him from within a small cave. The ground rose as he advanced, and when he emerged the trees had thinned.

His way took him to the left then, continuing uphill. He mounted higher and higher until he came at last to stand atop a ridge commanding a large view of the countryside. There he halted, staring into the black north, into which his trail ran on and on for as far as he could see in the odd half-light which had accompanied him on this journey. Opening his pouch, he cast pollen before him onto it. Turning then to the blue south, way to the earth-opening from which he had emerged, he cast more pollen, noticing for the first time that there was no trail behind him, that his way to this place had been vanishing even as he walked it. He felt that he would be unable to take a step in that direction if he were to try. There was to be no return along the way that he followed.

He faced the yellow west, place where the day was folded and closed. Casting pollen, he thought about endings, about the closing of cycles. Then to the east, thinking of all the mornings he had known and of the next one which would come out of it. Seeing for a great distance into the east with unusual clarity, he thought of the land over which his vision moved, adding features from the internal landscape of memory, wondering why he had ever wished to deny this Dinetah which was so much a part of him.

For how long he looked into the east he could not tell. Suddenly the air about his head was filled with spinning motes of light accompanied by a soft buzzing sound. It was like a swarm of fireflies dancing before him. Abruptly they darted off to his right. He realized then that it was a warning of some sort.

He looked to the right. There was a green glow moving among the trees in the distance. He looked away, placing his gaze upon his trail once again, and then he moved off along it.

Shortly he was running, ice particles stinging his face, driven by gusts of wind which raised them in occasional brief clouds. The snow did not obscure the trail, however. It was visible through everything with perfect clarity. Continuing to follow it into the distance with his eyes, he saw that it ran into an arroyo twisting off to the left. It seemed to narrow as it entered that place. Following, he saw that the narrowing continued until it appeared the thinness of a Christmas ribbon toward the center of the declivity. Strangely, however, the portion he was traversing appeared no narrower, though he knew that he had already reached and passed beyond the place where the thinning had begun. Instead, he detected a new phenomenon.

At first it was only that the arroyo had seemed somewhat deeper and longer than his initial impression had indicated. As he moved more deeply into it, however, the place itself seemed larger, a huge canyon with high walls. And the farther he progressed, the steeper the walls became, the greater the distance from wall to wall. It also was now strewn with massive boulders which had not been apparent at first. Yet the red way he followed remained undiminished. There were no signs of the contraction he had noticed earlier.

An enormous white wheel flew past him, sculpted and brilliant, five-limbed like a starfish. Immediately another moved slowly overhead, descending. He realized that it was a snowflake.

The place was larger than Canyon del Muerto, much larger. In moments, its walls had receded into the distance, vanished. He increased his pace, running, leaping, among the huge rocks.

He topped a rise to discover a massive glassy mountain looming before him, its prismatic surfaces retailing rainbows at peculiar angles.

Then he was descending toward it, and he could see where his trail ran into a large opening in its side, a jagged slash-mark through stone and sheen, like a black lightning bolt running from about a third of its height downward to the earth.

A gust of wind blew him over and he regained his footing and ran on. A snowflake crashed to the earth like a falling building. He raced across the top of a small pond which vibrated beneath him.

The mountain towered higher, nearer. Finally he was close enough to see into the great opening, and he saw that it shone within as well as without, the walls sparkling almost moistly, rising in a pitched-tentlike fashion to some unseen point of convergence high overhead.

He rushed within and halted almost immediately. His hand went to his knife before he realized that the men who surrounded him were multiple images of himself reflected in the gleaming walls. And his trail running off in all directions . . . Twisted images.

He bumped into a wall, ran his hands down its surface. His trail seemed to go straight ahead here, but he saw now where the real only seemed to join the illusory. It slid to the right, he could tell now.

Three paces and he bumped into another wall. This could not be. There was nothing else for the trail to do. It proceeded directly ahead here, with no deviations, reflected or otherwise.

He reached forward, felt the wall, searched it. His reflection mimicked his movements.

Abruptly, there was nothing. His hand moved forward as he realized that only the upper portion of his way was blocked. He dropped to all fours and continued onward.

As he crawled, the reflections shifted in the shadows around him. For a moment, from the corner of his eye, to the right, it seemed that he was a slow, lumbering bear, pacing himself. He glanced quickly to the left. A deer, a six-pointer, dark eyes alert, nostrils quivering. Multiple reflections caused them all to merge then, into something

197

that was bear and deer and man, something primeval, working its way, like First Man, through narrow, dark tunnels upward to the new world.

The reflections ahead showed him that the overhead space was growing larger again, turning into a high, narrow, Gothic arch. He rose to his feet as soon as he noticed this, and the animal images slipped away, leaving nothing but the infinity of himself on all sides. All colors, in various intensities, lay ahead. He went on, and when he saw that he was heading toward a way out, he began to run.

The area of light seemed to grow slightly smaller as he advanced upon it. The reflections which ran beside him now varied through prisms and shadows. And he noted that they were all differently garbed. One bounded along in a pressurized suit, another in a tuxedo; another wore only a loincloth. One ran nude. Another wore a parka. One had on a blue velveteen shirt he had long forgotten, a sandcast concho belt binding it above the hips. In the distance, he saw himself as a boy, running furiously, arms pumping.

Smiling, he ran out through the opening, along the red way. The canyon walls appeared and closed in on him, diminishing in height as he advanced.

He halted and looked back.

There was no shining mountain. He retraced his steps a dozen paces and stooped to pick up a piece of stone containing a cracked quartz crystal which lay on the ground. He held it up to his eyes. A rainbow danced within it. He dropped it into his pocket, feeling as if it held half of time and space.

He ran for nearly an hour then, and ice crystals scratched like the claws of cats at rocks and tree limbs, at his face. The frozen earth made noises like crinkling cellophane beneath his feet. Streaks of snow lay like crooked fingers on the hillsides. A patch of sky lightened and thunder rumbled nearby. His way led into the mountains, and soon he began to climb.

• • •

When I call,
they come to me

out of Darkness Mountain.
  Pipelines cross it,
  satellites pass above it,
  but I hold the land before me,
  and all things that hunt
  and are hunted within it.
  I have followed the People
  across the eons,
  giving the proper hunter his prey
  in the proper time.
Those who hunt themselves,
however, fall into a special category.
Certain sophistications were unknown
in ancient times.
But you are never too old to learn,
which is what makes this business interesting
and keeps me black-winged. Na-ya!
Out of Darkness Mountain, then:
Send an ending.

       • • •

And climbing, Everything strange. He had lost track of time and space. Sometimes the countryside seemed to roll by him, other times it seemed that he had moved for ages to cover a small distance. The trail took him among more mountains. He was no longer certain as to precisely where he was, though he was sure that he was still heading north. The snow turned into rain. The rain came and went. The trail led upward once again and moved through rocky passages. In places, streamlets rushed by him, and he passed through narrow necks with his back pressed against stone, fingertips and heels his only purchase. The clouds were occasionally delineated by a bright scribbling, to be wiped away by the grayness moments later.

  He passed through an opening so narrow that he had to strip off his pack and jacket and go sideways. It cut sharply to the left, and he knew that he could have missed it even in full daylight without the guiding trail that led him on. Glowing forms seemed to writhe in crevasses he passed before the way widened again, like the mating movements of the tall, spindly anklavars on the world called Bayou.

When he turned and stretched his cramped muscles, he halted. What was this place? There was a ruin built into the cliff face to the right. Farther ahead there was another, to the left and higher, at a place where the canyon continued its widening. Stone and rotted adobe, they were ruins with which he was not familiar, though he had once thought that he was aware of almost all of them. He was tempted to pause for a quick investigation, but the drumbeat commenced again, slowly, and his trail ran on to greater heights.

The canyon turned to the right, its floor rising even farther, its walls spread wider. He climbed, and there were more ruins about. The name "Lukachukai" passed through his mind as he remembered the story of a lost Anasazi ruin. The wind grew still and the pulse of the drum quickened. Shadowy shapes darted behind broken walls. He stared at the high, level place before him. He saw the end of his trail. A chill passed over his entire body, and he felt the hairs rise on the nape of his neck.

He took a step forward, then another. He moved cautiously, slowly, as if the ground might give way beneath him at any point. It was right, though, wasn't it? Of course. All trails end the same way. Why should this one be any different? If you tracked anything through its entire life, from its first faltering step until its final faltering step, the end was always the same.

Back beside a rock, beneath an overhang, his trail ended before the vacant gaze of an age-browned human skull. Beyond that, he could not see the way.

The rhythm of the drumbeat changed. *Mah-ih*, the Trickster, Coyote, He-who-wanders-about, peered at him from beyond the corner of a nearby ruin. A white rainbow *yei* formed an arc from the top of one canyon wall to the other. He heard the shaking of rattles now, accompanying the drumbeat. A green stem poked through the ground, rose upward, put forth leaves and then a red flower.

He walked on. As he advanced, the skull seemed to jerk slightly forward. A flickering occurred within it, and then a pale green light grew behind all of its apertures which faced him. Far off to the right, Coyote made a sudden, low, growling sound.

As he neared the end of the trail the skull tipped backward and turned slightly to the right, keeping the eyesockets fixed directly upon him.

A rasping voice emerged from the skull:

"Behold your *chindi.*"

Billy halted.

"I used to play soccer," he said, smiling and drawing back his foot. "Those two rocks up by the ruin can be the goal posts."

The ground erupted before him. The skull shot upward to a position perhaps a foot higher than his head. It rode upon the shoulders of a massive, nude, male body which had grown up like the flower before him. The green light danced all around it.

"Shadow-thing!" Billy said, unslinging his weapon.

"Yes. Your shadow. Shoot if you will. It will not save you."

Billy continued the movement which brought the snub-gun forward, reversing it in his hands, driving its butt hard upward against the skull. With a brief crunching noise the skull shattered, and its pieces fell to the ground. The trunk beneath dropped to one knee and the arms shot forward. A massive hand caught hold of the weapon and tore it from Billy's grasp. It cast it backward over its shoulder, to fall with a clatter among rocks far up the canyon and to vanish there.

The left hand caught his right wrist and held it with a grip like a steel band. He chopped at the other's biceps with the edge of his left hand. It had no apparent effect, and so he drew his hunting knife, cross-body, and plunged it into the headless one, in the soft area below the left shoulder joint.

Suddenly his wrist was free and the thing before him was falling backward, knees folding up toward the chest, arms clasping them.

Billy watched as the other rolled away, darkening, losing features, growing compact, making crunching noises in passing over gravel and sand. It had become a big, round boulder, slowing now. . . .

It came to a halt perhaps fifteen meters distant, and then, slowly, it

201

began to unfold into a new form. It unwound limbs and shaped a head, a tail . . .

An eye.

Cat stood facing him across the canyon of the lost city.

We shall continue where we left off before the interruption, he said.

MERCY SPENDER WAS JERKED OUT OF a deep, dreamless sleep. She began to scream, but the cry died within her. There was a twisted familiarity to what was happening. She drew herself into a fetal position and pulled the blankets up over her head.

Alex Mancin was spinning figures across his video console when it hit. When his vision wavered and dimmed, he thought that he was having a stroke. And then he realized what was happening and did not resist it, for his curiosity was stronger than his fear.

Elizabeth Brooke twisted from side to side. It was getting better every second. In just a few more moments . . . Her mind began to twist also, and she shrieked.

Fisher was in communication with Ironbear when the mental storm broke and they were sucked into another state of awareness.

What the hell is it? he asked.

We're being pulled back together again, Ironbear replied.

Who's doing it?

Sands. Can't you feel him? Like a broken lodestone, reassembling itself—

Nice image. But I still don't under— Ah!

Plosion ex. Im noisolp.

ashes falling back into bonfire, fireflame along the

202

across the night arcing east drawn tgthr brainbow four containing
ffth reassembling spring pushing upward beneath erth snows clds
sorting moisture bright spikes fllng waters flwng hllw-eyd ruins
facing knifemanhanded and rockdreamt beast lost within this place
of old ones weeeeI frthgo endlessly unwrapping thoughtveiling
countereal ity downow bhind substances tessences and above
fireflame waterflow and blow weI flsh the toilet of the world and let
the spiral remain powr now the pwr ander seav nightebbing kraft
tofil manshadow in shdworld he travel and wI the fireflame Iwe like
blude tofil circulate and recur along the manform outreach hmsel
   fireflame along the
   plosion

H E STANDS, CROUCHING, BLADE IN HIS
left hand. He moves the weapon slowly, turning it, raising it, lowering it, hoping for a glint or two to catch the vision behind the eye.
The beast takes a step forward. The green light is trapped within the
facets of that eye. Whether the blade holds any fascination for it he
cannot tell.

The beast takes another step.

A gentle rain is falling. He is uncertain when it commenced again.
It increases slightly in intensity.

Another step . . .

His right hand moves to his belt buckle and catches hold of it. He
turns to extend his left shoulder, continuing the movements of the
blade.

Another step . . .

The beast's tongue darts once, in and out. Something is not right.

203

Size? Pattern of movement? The cold absence of projected feelings when it had communicated?

Another step.

Still a little too far to spring yet, he decides. He turns his body a little more. He releases the belt buckle and slides his hand farther to his left, the movement masked by the flap of his jacket, by the angle at which he now stands. Is it reading his mind at this moment? He begins the Blessingway chant again, mentally, to fill his thoughts. Something inside him seems to take it up. It runs effortlessly within his breast, the accompanying feelings flowing without exertion.

Another . . .

Soon. Soon the rush. His right hand comes upon the butt of the tazer. His fingers wrap about it.

Almost . . .

Two more steps, he decides.

One . . .

Now is the time of the cutting of the throat . . .

Two.

He draws the weapon and fires it. It strikes home and the beast halts, stiffens.

He drops the tazer, snatches the knife into his right hand and lunges forward.

He halts several paces before the creature, for it begins melting and turning to steam. In moments, the form has dissolved and the vapors have collected into a small cloud about three meters above the ground. Lowering the knife, he raises his eyes.

Smokelike, it now drifts, passing to the left toward a huge pile of rubble from some ancient landslide. He follows, watching, waiting.

Neat trick, that.

I am not the beast you slew. I am that which you cannot destroy. I am all of your fears and failings. And I am stronger now because you fled me.

I did not flee you. I followed a trail.

What trail? I saw no trail save your own.

204

It is the reason I am in this place, and I presume I am the reason you are here.

The smoke ceases its movement, to hover above the rock heap.

Of course. I am the part of yourself which will destroy you. You have denied me for too long.

The smoke begins to contour itself into a new form.

I no longer deny you. I have faced the past and am at peace with it.

Too late. I have become autonomous under the conditions you created.

De-autonomize, then. Go back where you came from.

The form grows manlike.

I cannot, for you are at peace with the past. Like Cat, I have only one function now.

Cat is dead.

. . . And I lack a sense of humor.

The form continues its coalescence. Billy regards an exact double of himself, similarly garbed, holding a knife the exact counterpart of his own, looking back at him. It is smiling.

Then how can you be amused?

I enjoy my one function.

Billy raises the point of his blade.

Then what are you waiting for? Come down and be about it.

The double turns and leaps to his left, landing on the farther side of the heap. Billy rushes around it, but by the time he reaches him the other has regained his footing. He wipes his brow with his free hand, for the rain still descends. Then he drops into a crouch, both hands extended, low, knees bent. The other does the same.

Billy backs away as the other advances, then shuffles to his right, feinting, beginning the circle. He studies the ground quickly, hoping to steer the other into a slippery place. As his eyes move, his double lunges. He blocks with his left forearm and thrusts for the body. The point of the other's blade pierces his jacket sleeve and enters his arm. He is certain his own blade has bitten deeply into his adversary's left side, but the double gives no sign of it and Billy sees no blood.

205

"I am beginning to believe you," he says aloud, feeling his own blood dampen his arm. "Perhaps I cannot kill you."

"True. But I can kill you," the other replies. "I will kill you."

Billy parries the blade, slashes the other's cheek. No wound opens. No blood appears.

"So why do you not give up?" the other says.

"Supposing I were to throw down my knife and say to hell with it?" he asks.

"I would kill you."

"You say you will kill me whether I fight or do not fight?"

"Yes."

"Then I might as well fight," Billy says, thrusting again, parrying again, slashing low, moving back, thrusting high, circling.

"Why?"

"Warrior tradition. Why not? It's the best fight around."

As he backs away from a fresh attack, Billy almost stumbles when his right foot strikes an apple-sized stone. But he recovers and brushes it backward as if it were an annoyance. He slashes and thrusts furiously then, halting the other. Then he takes a big step back, positioning his foot just *so*. . . .

He kicks the stone as hard as he can, directly toward his double. It flies as from a catapult, striking the other's right kneecap with a satisfying *thunk*.

The figure bends forward, blade lowering. His head falls into a tempting position and Billy swings his left fist as hard as he can against the right side of his adversary's jaw.

The double falls back onto his left side, and Billy kicks again, toward the knife hand. His boot makes contact and the blade goes clattering across rocks into the distance. He flings himself upon the fallen form, his own blade upraised.

As he drives the blade downward toward the other's throat, his adversary's left hand flies up and the fingers wrap around his wrist. His arm stops as if it has encountered a wall. The pressure on his wrist is enormous. Then the right hand rises and he knows somehow that it is about to go for his throat.

He drives another left against the other's jaw. The head rolls to the side and the grip on his wrist slackens slightly. He strikes again and again. Then he feels a powerful movement beneath him.

His adversary bunches his legs, leans forward and begins to rise, bearing Billy along with him. He strikes again, but it seems to make no difference. The other's movement carries them both to their feet and that right hand is coming forward again. Billy seizes the extending wrist and barely manages to halt it. He pushes as hard as he can but he is unable to advance his knife hand.

Then, gradually, his left hand is forced back. His right wrist feels as if it is about to snap.

"You *chindis* are strong sons of bitches," he says.

The other snarls and flexes his fingers. Billy drives his knee into his groin. The double grunts and bends forward. Billy's knife advances slightly.

But as the other bends forward, Billy sees over him, beyond him. And he begins singing the song the old man taught him, the calling of Ikne'etso, the Big Thunder, recalling now when he had transferred power from the sandpainting to his own hand.

Sees . . .

First, to where the totem stands—the same four figures below; but now, crowning the spirit pole, the shadowy fifth form has grown more distinct and is shining with an unearthly glow. It seems to be smiling at him.

You have, I see, gambled. Good, it seems to say, and then the pole begins to elongate, stretching toward the now brightened heavens. . . .

To where, second, the rainbow now arches in full spectrum.

And his gaze continues to mount, to the rainbow's crest. There he sees the Warrior Twins regarding him as on that occasion so long ago. A dark form circles above them.

Nayenezgani strings his great bow. He puts an arrow to it, draws it partway back and begins to raise it. The dark form descends, and Black-god comes to sit upon Nayenezgani's shoulder.

The double tightens his grip and twists, and the knife falls from Billy's hand. He can feel the blood running up his left arm as the strength begins to ebb and the other draws him nearer. He continues to utter the words of the song, calling. . . .

The pole stands to an enormous height now, and the figure atop it—now a man from the waist up—is raising his right hand and lowering his left, pointing at him. He is reaching, reaching. . . .

The drumbeat grows louder, comes faster. The rattling sounds like a hailstorm.

Despite a final effort to thrust him back, the double stands his ground and draws Billy into a crushing embrace. But Billy continues to choke out the words.

Nayenezgani draws his bowstring all the way back, releases the arrow with a forward snapping motion of his left arm.

The world explodes in a flash more brilliant than sunlight. In that moment he knows that he has entered his double and his double has entered him, that he has fused with the divided one, that the pieces of himself, scattered, have come home, have reassembled, that he has won. . . .

And that is all that he knows.

✴⇒ *The Fourth Day* ⇐✴

Disk IV

BANK OF NOVA SCOTIA COMPUTER PLEADS NOLO CONTENDERE

STRAGEAN TRADE AGREEMENT NEARER REALITY

Roger Zelazny

DOLPHINS SETTLE OUT OF COURT

ILI REPORTS MISSING METAMORPH

• • •

Now you travel your own trail, alone.
What you have become, we do not know.
What your clan is now, we do not know.
Now, now on, now, you are something not of this world.

• • •

NEW YORK PHILHARMONIC TO PREMIERE "LEVIATHAN" SYMPHONY

Charlie, an aged humpback whale who makes his home in Scammon Lagoon, will hear the first instrumental performance of his composition via a satellite hookup to full-fidelity underwater speakers. Although he has refused to comment on the rehearsals, Charlie seemed

TAXTONIES DO IT AGAIN

When their leader's clone's bullet-riddled body was found in the East River, a potential riot situation was only temporarily averted

SMUDGE POTS IN VOLCANO CRATER CAUSE PANIC
ALIENS REPRIMANDED

210

A pair of tourists from Jetax-5, whose culture is noted for its eccentric sense of humor, admitted to

GENERAL ACCEPTS NOBEL PEACE PRIZE

. . .

crawling, he made it into a sheltered place. He leaned his back against a wall and dipped his finger into the blood. Reaching out

. . .

WHOOPING CRANE FLOCKS TO BE PRUNED

Hunting permits will be issued to deal with the overpopulation problem in flocks of the once rare crane which has now become a nuisance.

"Who can sleep with all that whooping?" complained residents

BERSERK FACTORY DESTROYS OUTPUT
HOLDS OFF NATIONAL GUARD FOR 8 HOURS
HOSTAGES RELEASED UNHARMED

. . .

There was an old bugger from Ghent
Spilled his drink in the sexbot's vent.
He screamed and he howled
As if disemboweled.
Instead of coming, he went.

. . .

COMPUTER THERAPIST CHARGED WITH MALPRACTICE

BLACK HOLE TO BE AUCTIONED

Roger Zelazny

At Sotheby Parke Bernet next Wednesday

A WET SPRING FOR MUCH OF THE NATION

                           t otempl fllng across beside the waters andown theating of thearth after fireflow fromigh wright but rong oh sands the merger each with sands sands sands sands ourglass runneth over days roulette struck fire andown thever narrowing tunnels of being we go fireflow part a part freverdreaming newslvs dreams tove touched the shaman mind beneath the bead fireflow across the windrawn days andown conditions of being focused through fireflood lens anew the hunted self achieved rainwet snowblow windcut daythrust knifeslash fireflown are the hunted and hunting selves the landscape dreamspoken nder earth of mind through heart of stars toth still the running the burgeoning the everrun foreverrun one frevermore as lps that kss the lightning creationheat everflow firetotem apart a part one frever and run

Mercy Spender, awakening with a taste for tea and the desire to attend a dog race—strange thought—called Fisher and asked him to join her in the dining room. Then she showered, dressed, combed her hair and thought about makeup for the first time since her early singing days.

Fisher rummaged through his thoughts, wondering whether his illusions could use a touch more class. How long since he had been to an art gallery? Studied himself in the mirror. Perhaps he ought to let his hair grow longer.

Out the window, new day clearing, snow melting, water dripping. He hummed a tune—Ironbear's, now he thought of it. Not bad, that beat.

Alex Mancin decided to undertake a retreat at a monastery he had heard of in Kentucky. The money market could take care of itself, and the dogs would be fed and groomed by the kennel keeper, poor bastard. They were such stupid little things.

Ironbear turned and sidled, passing through the narrow, rock-fallen place between sheer rises. As he had progressed, his ability to read the trail signs had grown better and better, exceeding perhaps what it had been in those long-forgotten days in the Gateway to the Arctic. Now, as he entered the canyon, he felt that he was nearing the trail's end.

He did not pause to study the ruins about him but moved directly to the area amid charred brush and grasses where the ground indicated that a struggle had occurred. He squatted and remained unmoving for a long while when he reached it, studying the earth. Chips of turquoise, dried blood . . . Whatever had gone on here had been very violent.

Finally he rose and turned toward the ruin to his left. Something had crawled or been dragged in that direction. He opened his mind and probed carefully but could detect nothing.

Vague images passed through his awareness as he approached the ruin. He had been present as part of the being which the Sands construct had formed here under highly symbolic circumstances, had felt the telekinetic power reaching, felt the blast. But after that event, nothing. He was swept away at that very point, to continue his tracking.

. . . And then he saw him, propped against a wall near a corner of the ruin. At first Ironbear could not tell whether he was breathing, though his eyes were open and directed to his right.

Moving nearer, he saw the pictograph Singer himself had drawn on the wall with his own blood. It was a large circle, containing a

213

pair of dots, side by side, about a third of the way down its diameter. Lower, beneath these, was an upward-curving arc.

Inhaling the moment, Ironbear shook his head at what was rare, at what was powerful. Like the buffalo, it probably would not last. A life's gamble. But just now, just this instant, before he advanced and broke the feeling's spell, there was something. Like the buffalo.

> *High on the mountain of fire*
> *in the lost place of the Old Ones,*
> *fire falling to the right of me,*
> *to the left of me,*
> *before, behind, above, below,*
> *I met my self's* chindi,
> chindi's *self.*
> *Shall I name me a name now,*
> *to have eaten him?*
>
> *I walk the rainbow trail.*
> *In a time of ice and fire*
> *in the lost place of the Old Ones*
> *I met my self's* chindi,
> *became my* chindi's *self.*
> *I have traveled through the worlds.*
> *I am a hunter in all places.*
> *My heart was divided into four parts*
> *and eaten by the winds.*
> *I have recovered them.*

214

I sit at the center of the entire world
sending forth my song.
I am everywhere at home,
and all things have been given back to me.
I have followed the trail of my life
and met myself at its end.
There is beauty all around me.

Nayenezgani came for me
into the Darkness House,
putting aside with his staff
the twisted things, the things reversed.
The Dark Hunter remembers me,
Coyote remembers me,
the Sky People remember me,
this land remembers me,
the Old Ones remember me,
I have remembered myself
coming up into the world.
I sit on the great sand-pattern
of Dinetah, here at its center.
Its power remembers me.

Coyote call across the darkness bar . . .
I have eaten myself and grown strong.
There is beauty all around me.
Before me, behind me, to the right
and to the left of me,
corn pollen and rainbow.
The white medicine lifts me in his hand.

The dancer at the heart of all things
turns like a dust-devil before me.
My lightning-bead is shattered.
I have spoken my own laws.

215

My only enemy, my self, reborn,
is also the dancer.
My trail, my mind, is filled with stars
in the great wheel of their turning
toward springtime. Stars.
I come like the rain with the wind
and all growing things.
The white medicine lifts me in his hand.
Here at lost Lukachukai I say this:
The hunting never ends.
The way is beauty.
The medicine is strong.
The ghost train doesn't stop here
anymore. I am the hunter
in the eye of the hunted. If I call
they will come to me
out of Darkness Mountain.

ABOUT THE AUTHOR

Roger Zelazny was born in Cleveland, Ohio, graduated from Western Reserve University and went to Columbia University for a master's degree. He worked for the Social Security Administration in Cleveland and then in Baltimore until he quit to begin writing full-time in 1969.

His first appearances in the field were short stories with his earliest story of note being "A Rose for Ecclesiastes." Shortly thereafter he won the first of his several Hugo and Nebula awards, the Hugo for. . . *And Call Me Conrad* (later published in book form as *This Immortal,* 1966) and two Nebulas in the same year for "He Who Shapes" (later expanded and published in book form as *The Dream Master,* 1966) and "The Doors of His Face, The Lamps of His Mouth." Two years later he won the Hugo Award again for his most famous novel *Lord of Light* (1967). He has continued to produce a body of significant work in the shorter lengths, winning both the Nebula and Hugo awards for best novella for "Home Is the Hangman," while producing many popular novels including the five-volume "Amber" series beginning with *Nine Princes in Amber* in 1970 and concluding with *The Courts of Chaos* in 1978.

Although sometimes associated with the New Wave movement popular in science fiction circles at the time when he first began publishing, especially because of the richness of his imagery and his poetically charged style, Zelazny has always been truly independent of literary movements, perpetually creating interesting and exciting stories and telling them in his own way.

Zelazny lives in Santa Fe, New Mexico, with his wife and three children—two sons and a daughter.